Voices

A Novella

Kayla Frederick

Editing by S.K. Gregory
Cover Art by BetiBup33 /
https://thebookcoverdesigner.com/designers/betibup33/

First Edition January 2024
ISBN: 978-1-950530-36-6

Chapter One

Lynn

"LOONY LYNN!" A kid on a bike screamed at the woman standing beside the curb.

No emotion flickered across her face, but she gripped her suitcase tighter.

Loony Lynn.

That was a nickname she hadn't heard in some time. Unpleasant nostalgia washed over her like a slap across the face, and she considered flagging down the cab that had brought her here. Would it be enough to go back? If only she had the power.

Lynn stared the boy down as he did a circle in the road, sticking his tongue out for effect. Lynn watched him, not responding, but also not looking away. She used to be sharper, and quick-witted. People who called her names before regretted it.

Before, she reminded herself of the keyword, watching the boy ride away.

A house with brown siding and a big wooden porch sat a few yards away. The screen door creaked open, and Lynn's mother, Catherine, stepped onto the porch, hands on her hips to study the yard and the person responsible for destroying her peace.

When she caught sight of her daughter, she squealed

and rushed to her, no regard for her lack of shoes or the array of pine needles scattered across the walkway. When she reached Lynn, she cupped her face in her hands, offering no hope for escape.

"Sweet Pea! I'm so happy to see you," she said with an accent somewhere between Southern and none at all. "I wasn't expecting you until Saturday! Why didn't you call?"

"Figured it'd be more of a surprise this way," Lynn said, pulling subtly out of her mother's grip. "I got the money together and thought there was no use in waiting."

Her mother beamed, but Lynn barely saw it. In the back of her mind flashed the giant red *F* that had been stamped on her midterms. Her first semester of college, she'd been a resounding failure, which came as an even bigger letdown considering all the work she'd put into being admitted. She'd counted her blessings for the opportunity, jumping through every hoop. Now, her second semester was turning out worse.

The wooden porch steps creaked under their weight, announcing their movements all the way to the door. Catherine had left it wide open, exposing the kitschy wallpaper and plain brown furniture inside. A giant potted fern sat to the right and an empty coat rack to the left. Lynn nearly knocked it over in her hurry to close the door, grateful to block out the nasty neighbor boy who leered from the road as he pedaled past the house again. He'd put in work to be here.

Hell, Michigan was an original place in every sense

of the word. Officially, it wasn't a *town* since only about a hundred people resided there, but it had a store, diner, post office, and of course plenty of tourist attractions.

For the most part, the town was one big, running joke. The history behind the name always made Lynn laugh. Two rumors competed for acknowledgment. One - the town came about its name because the founder, when asked what he'd like to name his town, responded with *"You can call it Hell for all I care."* The second rumor involved alcoholic husbands and catty wives.

Lynn liked to believe that both rumors held some weight. It was what gave the place its delightful *charm* as her mother called it.

Lynn could go either way. For such a large portion of her life, she'd dreamed of leaving her sleepy little town and traveling to the big city. She yearned for the hustle and bustle, to be swept up by it all and spit out a strong, successful woman.

Instead, you failed, a sharp biting thought penetrated her mind. She slapped the side of her head, trying to make it stop.

Catherine frowned, eyeing her with a look of careful concern that only mothers could ever perfect. "Have you been taking your medication?"

"Of course. Not that it helps," Lynn replied, plucking the bottle from her pocket to show off the few remaining pills.

Catherine's expression tightened. "If they're really

not working, it might be time to visit Dr. Phillip again."

Lynn struggled to hold her tongue. So far Dr. Philip *hadn't* found a medication that really helped her and changing it again meant admitting defeat. She kept the thought to herself, knowing Catherine would get her way in the end.

She always did.

"Go on and get unpacked. Amelia will be here tomorrow," Catherine said, eyes shining as if the thought of her nest being full again brought her nothing but joy. The expression dimmed slightly when Lynn's face didn't change. "She's excited to see you, you know? She must've called fifty times this week to check up on you."

Lynn raised her eyebrows, surprised by the news. Logically, she should've figured out her sister would also want to visit, but the information still made her skin crawl. Amelia had always been the perfect daughter. Catherine had never called Lynn a failure outright, but she could see the unspoken words in her mother's eyes when she spoke of her favorite daughter.

"Amelia's coming?" Lynn asked, at last, feigning as much interest as she could.

"Of course," Catherine said, a look of absolute adoration for her firstborn on her face.

"Fantastic," Lynn murmured and grabbed the handle of her suitcase so tight it hurt.

Welcome to Hell.

Chapter Two
Jayden

THE BACKSEAT OF Kasey's car was always comfortable and clean. *Too* clean as if Kasey had committed some atrocity that required a thorough scrubbing to get rid of any and all evidence. Jayden dug the heels of his hands into his eyes until he saw stars and slumped in the leather seat. He blinked them away and stared out the window. From the corner of his eye, he picked up a set of brown eyes peering at him in the rearview mirror.

"That's some hefty sighing you're doing back there, man," Kasey said.

Kay, a twenty-two-year-old wallflower with a bright blonde bob craned her neck to look at him over the top of her seat. "Everything okay?"

Jayden's eyes volleyed between them. Kasey and Kay, his two best friends. Except things weren't so straightforward anymore. They were the cart he dangled from as the third wheel. Their relationship hadn't started long ago, a few weeks at most, and as a result, they were in the early stages of infatuation. The kind that leaves a person unable to get enough of their sweetheart. The kind of love that made Jayden feel like a creep for being in their vicinity.

"Yeah, I'm fine. A little tired, but I mean it *is* noon already."

"Look," Kasey said slowly, dramatically. "If you don't want to go just say so. My feelings won't be hurt."

Jayden narrowed his eyes. Him tagging along might not hurt *Kasey's* feelings but to Jayden? The quick dismissal gutted him. He and his friends had lived in Michigan their entire lives and frequently heard the stories of the tourist pit of Hell, Michigan, but none of them had been able to go. Then Kasey had gotten the idea to go right before Halloween so they could say they spent Devil's Night in Hell with the devil.

In theory, it had been the perfect escape from classes and the drama of his parents forcing him to consider majors he wasn't interested in. Jayden turned his face toward the window, hoping his hurt didn't show. When he realized Kasey's eyes were still watching him, he painted on a smile full of fake enthusiasm. "No, man. This is gonna be great. I mean who doesn't want to spend a weekend in Hell?"

Kasey smiled. "Now *that's* the right attitude."

Kay frowned, full lips pushing out into the pout she used to get Kasey to bend to her whim. "Well, I don't know if I can spend the *entire* weekend there."

Jayden stared at the back of her head, sorting through conflicting feelings of the warmth their friendship used to hold and a new sense of loathing for her. He wasn't nearly as close to anyone else in the dorms as he was to these two, but suddenly he wondered if he'd have a better weekend staying home, playing with a Ouija board, and hooking up with a spooky girl.

"If that's the case, it's probably better we take different cars," Jayden said. "That way if anyone needs to leave," he paused long enough to pin the back of her head with a glare, "we can."

"But half the fun is the road trip!" Kasey protested, side-eyeing Jayden the best he could. "We can make terrible financial decisions on snacks that'll make us sick in two hours. It'll be great!"

Kay tossed him a sideways glare that said, *really*?

A real bummer, Jayden thought, hardly able to resist curling his lip.

Kasey looked back to the road, but the glimpse of his face that Jayden could see told him the moment had left him at least *mildly* upset by the change in plans. The road passed in a blur as Kasey turned onto the street that led to their dorms, halting beside the curb.

Jayden made a move to hop out.

"Wait!" Kasey stopped him, pulling a notebook out of the glove box. He jotted something down and tore the paper free, handing it to Jayden. "This is the name of the hotel. Meet us here when you make it, okay?"

Jayden tucked the paper into his pocket, hardly glancing at the squiggly lines. "Sure," he said. "See you guys later."

He slammed the door, trudging up toward the dorm. When the car started to move, he glanced over his shoulder long enough to realize that neither of his friends stared after him. Pushing his way into the building, he could think of nothing better than a long nap.

Chapter Three
Lynn

IN THE ISOLATION of her dorm, Lynn had missed her family. Her mother in particular. She'd had a list of things she'd wanted to do when she eventually returned home, but now that she was back, she remembered all the reasons she'd wanted to escape in the first place.

Lynn unpacked the most needed of her belongings and crawled into bed, falling asleep almost as soon as her head hit the pillow. When Amelia arrived early in the morning, Lynn was the first to know. Amelia could've had a fantastic career as a cat burglar with her quick steps and swift movements. She crept into Lynn's room, squeezing her into a bear hug without a fight from her still-sleeping sister.

The inside of Lynn's brain mushed with panic, and she tried to take in a deep breath, assuming the shadows in her room had reared up to suck the life out of her. When Amelia released her, she slunk backward, her silhouette illuminated by the early morning sun streaming in through the crack between the blinds and window sill. Even in the low light, Lynn could pick out the highlights in her hair and the healthy glow to her cheeks. College had been good to her.

"Jesus! Are you trying to give me a heart attack?" Lynn cried.

Amelia's smile grew somehow wider as she plopped down beside Lynn. "Nope. I'm excited to see my little sister again."

"Why?" Lynn asked, shoving her blanket toward Amelia to make some sort of divide between them. "Last time we were here, we tortured each other. Tradition is still going strong it seems."

"That's what siblings do. Don't gotta be so sensitive all the time," Amelia said, leaning in as if she were sharing some great secret.

"Yeah, well, you don't gotta be so perfect all the time either, but here we are."

"Whatever. Mom loves us the same. And you know why? Because *both* of us are gonna take over the world one day."

Lynn looked away, staring off into the corner of the room. How could she be the ruler of anything when she couldn't even keep *herself* in check?

"What is it?" Amelia asked. "Don't tell me you hate college already."

Lynn's face drew tight. *Had she really not heard?* Or was this a game to twist the knife in deeper? Lynn couldn't tell.

"I hate it," Lynn said at last. "I have no friends, and I can't understand most of my assignments. I'm failing three of my classes which means an extra semester of school if I want this degree. So I made the decision to withdraw. At least for this semester. It's so...humiliating."

Amelia frowned and tapped one perfectly manicured nail to the middle of Lynn's forehead. "Is it because of this?"

Lynn barely resisted the urge to slap her. "No. Not *because of that.*"

Truth was, she didn't want to try to pinpoint *what* could be the reason. Maybe it was the result of being somewhere strange, somewhere new, or maybe it was something psychological. Maybe it simply came down to the fact she wasn't as smart as she'd believed herself to be.

"Well, whatever the case, you're here now, and I'm glad to see you," Amelia said, planting a kiss on the spot between Lynn's eyes that she'd carelessly jabbed earlier. "Mom really thought that once you got a taste of life in the big city, you'd be gone forever."

In another life, Lynn thought. "Wasn't as if I had much else to do," she said, admittedly uncomfortable with her sister's warmth.

"I'm determined to cheer you up today."

Lynn glared at her. "The best way to do that would've been to *not* wake me up with a heart attack."

"Well, how else could I get your attention? Not as if you ever call me back. Now, we can spend the whole day together. Get some ice cream or something."

"You think hanging out in those tourist traps is a good time?" Lynn said, rolling her eyes. Amelia's expression didn't change, and Lynn laughed. "Fine. We can go."

Amelia mock-punched her sister in the arm and left the room to give Lynn the privacy to change. Lynn ruffled her hair and threw on a t-shirt and pants, pulling her favorite black shirt on top, before brushing her curly black locks and following her sister downstairs.

Catherine had finished setting places for them at the dining room table. The scent of bacon made her mouth water.

"Smells good, Mom," Lynn said, pulling out the nearest chair.

Amelia sat beside her, staring at her plate with shining gratitude. Lynn picked up a piece of bacon, taking a bite of the savory meat when Catherine said, "Oh, Lord, we thank you for this blessing we're about to consume."

Lynn tried to stop chewing, to pretend she hadn't dug right in, but the rest of the bacon strip remained in her hand. Amelia side-eyed her, and Lynn lowered the piece back onto her plate, swallowing to get rid of the remaining traces of her crime.

"Amen," Catherine finished.

"Amen," Amelia echoed.

Lynn didn't even try. Greedily, she devoured the rest of the bacon, savoring the taste.

Catherine watched her and scooped up a clump of eggs. "What do you girls have planned today?"

"I thought we'd go into town," Amelia spoke up. "Maybe get some ice cream and catch up with everyone again."

"That sounds like a lovely idea," Catherine said, making eye contact with Amelia before moving on to Lynn.

Lynn wondered what the look meant, but the way her skin crawled left her with the certainty it was hope. Hope Lynn was recovering. Hope that someday Lynn would be normal like her God-like sister.

Out loud, Lynn said, "Yeah," and crammed a mouthful of eggs into her mouth so large Catherine winced.

"Didn't they feed you at that college?" she asked.

"Why?" Lynn asked, egg crumbles still dotted at the corners of her mouth.

"I thought you'd eat more like a lady and less like a snake," Catherine admitted.

"Sorry. It's been too long since I've had a meal that *doesn't* consist of soup and crackers," Lynn admitted.

"Didn't they have a café?"

"Yeah," Lynn said. "Problem with those though is that they usually require money."

"You could've asked me for some at any time."

Lynn didn't respond, knowing that to do so would only extend the conversation. The rest of the meal passed in silence, and Lynn was grateful. She didn't want to rehash her college experience any more than she had to.

Amelia set her fork on her plate with a *clink,* and Lynn looked at her, wiping her mouth with her napkin.

"Ready?"

Lynn scooped the last bite into her mouth. "Ready." She stood up so fast her chair scraped the floor.

"Be safe out there," Catherine called behind them as they raced into the living room like they were kids all over again.

Amelia snorted. "We're going right down the road. What does she think could happen?"

"We might go to Hell," Lynn said.

The sisters broke out into laughter.

As the sound died off, and Lynn slid into her boots with practiced ease, she said, "It's a mother's job to worry about her children. I don't know about you, but I'd be pretty offended if she *wasn't* worried."

Amelia held the door open for Lynn, and she stepped outside, glad to feel the fall breeze on her face.

"The air smells so much better here," Lynn said. The trees gave the sweetest aroma that hadn't existed in Ann Arbor. "In the city, it's almost..."

"Toxic?" Amelia guessed.

"Yeah. I know I haven't been away that long, but it feels like forever."

"I'm sure Mom would say the same thing."

Lynn shook her head. "That's the second time now you've mentioned Mom being worried about me. Why does everyone *worry* about me?"

Amelia struggled for words, eyes telling Lynn things she wouldn't like the words to if Amelia *did* manage to say them.

"I'm fine," she said before Amelia could find her sentence. "So *don't* worry."

"If you say so," Amelia said, not sounding sure in the least.

Lynn grumbled and shoved her hands in the pockets of her hoodie, the gesture comforting for an odd reason she couldn't pinpoint.

The early sun was nice and warm on their faces as they wandered down the long, dirt road. Amelia kept her eyes straight ahead, but Lynn couldn't help glancing back a few times. Their home had disappeared a few minutes prior, leaving only the woods surrounding them on either side of the road. She hadn't remembered the walk being so long before. Or creepy. When she glanced into the tree line, she could fool herself into believing someone stood in the shadows, staring back.

BY THE TIME Lynn and Amelia made it to the café, the sun sat at its highest point in the sky. Lynn was hot and tired and wished she would've brought a water bottle to quench her thirst. She didn't remember October being so warm before and wondered if Indian summer had come late this year. Beside her, Amelia seemed no worse for wear, and Lynn was more convinced that she simply wasn't human.

"Forget ice cream, I might go with ice water," Lynn grumbled as Amelia held open the door, gesturing for her to go inside.

"We didn't come all this way for you to sulk, girlie," Amelia said in her best *too bad* voice.

Knowing she wouldn't win the argument, Lynn went inside. The place wasn't packed by a normal town's standards, but for Hell, Michigan, it was busy. A group of tourists stood in line for ice cream, giggling at the names of the flavors. Lynn shot Amelia a sarcastic glance.

"Be nice. They don't see it every day like we do," she chastised.

Lynn bit her lip to keep from replying. It was the truth, but it didn't lessen how annoying it made it for her.

"Well, well, look who we've got here," the cashier, Darlene, said with her trademark crooked smile. "I haven't seen you two in ages."

"Big college years for both of us," Amelia said, hooking her arm over Lynn's shoulders. She smelled sweet of cotton candy and flowery body spray. "We're back to spend some time with Mom before all the holiday craziness."

Lynn gave her sister a grateful glance, melting into the gesture that had made her so uncomfortable earlier. She didn't know how many townsfolk knew the truth about her and her struggle, but she certainly didn't want to find out.

Darlene nodded. "That's sweet. You girls always were." She patted the top of the barrier covering the ice cream. "Speaking of sweet, can I get you two something?"

Amelia ordered two cones for them and pulled out her wallet before Lynn could even realize she'd left hers at home.

Darlene waved a hand at her. "Are you kidding? It's on the house."

"Thank you," Amelia said, an award-winning smile on her face as she took the cones, passing one to Lynn.

Lynn took it gratefully, not bothering to ask the flavor of the white and blue swirled ice cream. Glancing up, she caught the stare of one of the tourist men on her. Awkwardly, she slipped into the nearest empty seat with her back to him and licked the ice cream. The flavor nearly sang on her tongue and it took restraint to not wolf it down.

Amelia sat across from her, eating in small, dainty bites. Excess ice cream was immediately dabbed away. When half of Lynn's ice cream was gone, two of the tourists passed on their way out the door. Lynn risked a glance over her shoulder to the one who'd stared at her earlier and realized he was still there.

"Let's get out of here," she said, adjusting the cone so that a running drip of ice cream was caught in her napkin.

Amelia peered over her shoulder and caught on, agreeing. The café opened up to a large clearing ringed with trees. They did a lap around it, taking in the afternoon sun and finishing off their snacks. The forest air cleansed away all the pollution from the city, making Lynn feel fresh in a way she hadn't in a while. She popped the last bite of the cone into her mouth, and as she chewed, she stared into the shadows cast by the nearest line of trees, unable to pull her eyes away.

Find me, a tiny whisper crawled into her mind.

Like the opening of a gateway, it was followed by a thousand whispers so intense she clamped her hands over her ears, desperately trying to block it out.

It didn't work. The voices grew louder, angrier.

Amelia dropped her remaining bit of ice cream and hurried to her sister's side, trying to get her attention. "Lynn! Lynn! Look at me."

Lynn shut her eyes, worried she'd explode under the internal pressure if anything else stimulated her brain. When she thought she would scream, the voices stopped at once. Lynn blinked, squinting with the fear they would return. She dropped her hands, palms coated in a layer of blood.

Amelia gasped and looked up at Lynn as if she feared she'd faint. "Oh, my God. Are you okay?"

Lynn turned her hands, studying the way the blood glistened in the sunlight. "Y-yeah, I'm fine," she said, suddenly tired.

"Let's get you home so I can get you cleaned up," Amelia said, tugging Lynn's wrist gently to get her attention.

Lynn stared into the mouth of the woods for a heartbeat longer before she turned away. "Okay."

Chapter Four
Jayden

*R**ING. RING.*

Jayden jolted awake.

Ring. Ring.

The phone perched on the wall rung over and over again. Groggy, he fought through the haze long enough to slide out of bed and pick up Kasey's number on the answering machine. Then his eyes drifted to the clock in the corner.

A string of curses fell from him as he wiped the drool from his chin. He ignored Kasey's call and hurried to the bathroom, splashing water on his face and through his hair, flattening the messy dark locks before glancing up at his reflection. The water nearly ran off him, the brown spikes coming back up to contrast his pale skin. He adjusted the black 12mm gauges in his ears and the hoop ring on his bottom lip. All attempts to look tougher than he was. Scarier. From his appearance, most people would never guess that he cried over sappy movies and wore his heart on his sleeve. Jayden poked his lip ring with his tongue as he turned away from the mirror. Sometimes, it was still weird to think that the two biggest focal points of his appearance started with a dare.

The pager in Jayden's pocket buzzed as he left the

dorm. Jayden eyed the nearby payphone, debating if he should call but he decided not to worry about it. He hurried through the lot in a rush of black clothes and honking cars and made it to his own car at the back of the lot. It was small and unassuming, a hand-me-down from his older brother as a parting gift for college.

Jayden slipped into the driver's seat and tossed his pager to the side. He considered shutting it away in the glove box, knowing full well that in about ten minutes, Kasey would most likely try to call him again. He reconsidered when it hit him that he didn't *exactly* know where he was going. He'd never been outside of the city.

College had given him the hope that he'd get to explore a larger section of the world than this. Then reality struck him upside the head with the reminder that his family couldn't afford it, and he simply didn't make the grades to pull it off.

I can still enjoy myself without them, Jayden thought as the buildings and major roadways of the city faded into dirt roads and forests.

Just like a horror movie, he mused, studying the shadows of the towering pine trees. The winding dirt road led him deeper and deeper into the woods until even the scattered remote homes vanished. *I'm gonna die out here.*

When he started to think he'd be better off turning around and going home, the dirt road opened to a clearing. The shadowy outline of a building came into view, and he spotted some vehicles, one of them familiar. Jayden parked a few spaces away and walked over to the burnt orange sedan, knocking on the window.

Kasey rolled the window down, an unpleased expression on his face. From the passenger seat, Kay smiled in greeting, but Kasey's eyes went back to the steering wheel.

"Thought you were gonna flake on us," he grumbled. "Had us sitting here for an hour."

Jayden held his hands up apologetically. "I'm here now."

Kasey laughed, a short sharp bark that made Jayden wince. He'd been so convinced that *Kay* would be the one to ruin this trip that it hardly dawned on him that he could do it too. "Took a nap. Figured it wouldn't be good to drive if I was too tired to see straight." His gaze went to the plastic bag nestled beside Kay's thigh. "Looks as if you two haven't been sitting here, waiting for me."

Kasey side-eyed it but kept silent. Kay bobbed her head and tapped it. "The souvenir shops here are awesome. There's an ice cream place too but—"

"We were waiting for you," Kasey cut in.

Jayden raised his eyebrows, recognizing his sulking from hours before. "Cheer up, man. I'm here now. We can do whatever you want to do."

Kasey grabbed the handle, staring up at Jayden as he pushed the car door open. "I'm gonna hold you to that," he said and closed the door with a resounding thud as Kay took her place at his side.

Jayden made a grand sweeping motion toward the path. "Of course, master."

The steel on Kasey's face broke, and he snickered. "Okay, jackass."

Kay linked her arm through Kasey's as they began to walk toward the building. "I've heard some great things about this place."

"I don't need other people to recommend ice cream. I'll never *not* want ice cream," Kasey said, peering down at the phone.

Jayden shoved his hands in his pockets and walked by their side. "I wonder what flavors they've got."

"The mystery is half the fun," Kay said.

Jayden prodded his lip ring, holding open the door for them to walk through. He lagged behind, taking in the decor as Kasey and Kay approached the counter. Plastic flames and little devil faces had been pinned to the wall. The floor was eerily dark. Kay leaned toward the glass, reading the bold print.

Kay started to list the flavors, and Jayden zoned out. His trance was broken when the door opened, and two women shuffled in. One was tall with long blonde hair and the other was short with black curls and a scowl. His attention was drawn to her, to the intensity of her face as her eyes swept around the restaurant, at last meeting his gaze. Embarrassed he'd been caught staring, he ducked his gaze away.

"This is crazy," Kasey said, pulling Jayden's

attention away from the newcomer. The smile on his friend's face reminded him of prior years when they'd been younger, and life had been much more exciting than it was now. "What do you think you'll get?"

Jayden fidgeted with his lip ring again, side-eyeing the girl to find her attention had fallen off him, and was focused on the girl she'd come in with. "Something that won't get me sent to Hell preferably."

"Too late for that," Kasey said, raising his eyebrows. "But for my risk-taking friend, I think I'll go with the wildest thing they have and get you plain o' chocolate. If you can handle that."

"Guess we'll have to find out."

Kasey turned to the woman and recited their order. Jayden tried to keep focused on his group but couldn't resist the urge to sneak another peek across the room. The girl and her friend were engaged in conversation with the cashier.

Seems like they know each other, he noted. *Must be locals.*

He tried to imagine that. To grow up in a place so remote, so disconnected from the rest of the world. He liked to think he'd have a permanent scowl too.

An elbow nudged him in the ribs, and Jayden turned toward Kasey, startled.

"See something you like?" his friend teased.

Blushing, Jayden looked down at the floor, but Kay stared straight ahead, trying to gauge who he'd been looking at. "She's cute."

"So what? I think they're locals," Jayden murmured with a shrug, taking the ice cream from his friend's outstretched hand. "I was trying to imagine what it would be like to grow up here. It's so...quiet. Different from the city."

"Lonely and boring, I'd imagine," Kasey said and shoved a mouthful of ice cream into his mouth.

Kay scowled and handed him a napkin from the nearby dispenser. "I'd never be able to sleep here. I'd always think there was someone in the woods watching me. I mean…what is there even to do around here? No movie theaters, no malls, no bowling alleys. I'd hate to be stuck here long term."

Jayden was torn between agreeing and arguing. Something about the city got to him on his bad days. Everyone being crammed together and never being able to find a space to truly be alone wasn't one of his favorite things about home. Of course, he wasn't an outdoorsy person either, so miles of endless woods also weren't in his wheelhouse.

Kasey led the way to the nearest table and pulled out a chair for Kay before they sat down, Jayden slipping into the seat across the table. From his perspective, he could see out the window, at the road beyond. It was a highway, and yet, it was rare for anyone to actually drive past. The longer he watched, the more he started to believe this place existed to only a select few humans and was inaccessible to the rest of the world.

By the time Jayden tore his attention from the window, Kasey and Kay had their faces close together, engaged in a conversation he wasn't privy to. Their ice creams were mostly gone, and he'd barely touched his.

Kasey raised an eyebrow when he caught Jayden's eye. "Welcome back."

Jayden smirked and licked a drop of sticky chocolate from his cone.

"We're gonna go check out the chapel," Kay said, rising from her seat with a huge smile on her face.

Jayden twitched his nose. "Chapel...like for weddings?"

"Yes," Kay said. "Getting married in Hell means the only way we can go is up."

Kasey laughed with her, but Jayden couldn't bring himself to do the same. Young love really made his stomach twist.

"You guys have fun. I'll catch up later," Jayden said, holding up his cone. "I have a bit of work to finish here first."

Kasey narrowed his eyes. "And you'll meet up with us in a bit, right? Not gonna go back to the hotel without us?"

Jayden pulled his best serious face. "You have my sworn honor."

Kasey dug his knuckles into the top of Jayden's head when he passed, and Jayden watched the pair of them head out, past the girls at the other table. He'd be sure to meet up with them again, but only after he was sure their cutesy hijinks were long over.

Chapter Five
Lynn

LYNN DIDN'T KNOW where Catherine was when she and Amelia arrived back home, but Lynn was glad she wouldn't have to be interrogated. The blood on her hands had dried into a thick crust that flaked when she flexed her hands in and out of fists. Amelia hurried her into the bathroom to clean her up and needle her with questions.

"Has this happened before?" Amelia asked, crumpling up the last wad of bloody tissue paper to toss in the trashcan.

It hadn't. Neither had the surge of voices, but Lynn didn't want to tell Amelia that. She didn't want to tell *anyone* that. With it would come the unpleasant assumption that she was getting crazier.

Who's to say you're not? an ugly little voice jeered. She didn't recognize it.

"Yeah, it has," she said when she snapped back to reality and realized Amelia still waited for an answer. To avoid seeing the look on her sister's face, she rose from her seat on the edge of the bathtub and tried to breeze past her.

Amelia took one step to the left, blocking the door. "Is the bleeding a side effect of your medicine?"

Lynn barely suppressed the urge to roll her eyes. To Amelia, every problem Lynn had was because of her mental illness. She could fall and break her arm, and Amelia would twist it back to what was going on in her head.

When Lynn had first been diagnosed with schizophrenia a few years back, she took it hard. The stigma of the illness was such a terrible thing to overcome, perhaps worse than the disease itself, and she'd dealt with it terribly. She thought about her friends, about Damien, about her perfect sister, and didn't want to accept the fact that out of all of them, *she* was the defect, the broken one. The one that simply didn't work.

Her condition wasn't something that could be ignored though. Even now, when she didn't want to think about it, she'd remember her first episode and cringe. Lynn had been in the kitchen, trying to make herself something to eat. Voices had whispered from somewhere behind the seasoning cabinet, and the closer she got, the more vicious those voices became.

She didn't remember picking up the knife, but she'd gotten one. A large meat cleaver that she'd held so wrong and so tight that she'd nearly severed several of her fingers. Luckily, Amelia had been passing by the kitchen and seen the knife. She pulled it from Lynn's hand before the damage could be too severe.

Lynn flexed her fingers, seeing the perfect white line that ran from her pointer finger to her third finger. Every time she saw the scar, she had no choice but to accept the validity of the medicine. After all, it had kept another such incident from happening.

Until now, of course.

"I don't know," Lynn huffed and tried to open the door again, nostrils flaring when Amelia still wouldn't budge.

Amelia folded her arms across her chest, giving her best motherly glare. "Let me see the bottle."

Lynn snorted. "I don't have it on me." She ducked around her sister and finally squeezed her way out of the bathroom.

Amelia followed a step behind, and Lynn's eye twitched. She wanted to be left alone, to decompress and try to understand what had happened without someone breathing down her neck, doing it for her.

"Everything alright, girls?" Catherine asked from the kitchen.

Judging by the worry in her voice, Lynn guessed she already knew *something* had happened.

"Yeah. Lynn had—"

"An urge to go back outside," Lynn interrupted, glaring at Amelia.

The conversation was most likely going to happen with or without her, but if she had a choice, she wasn't going to sit in on it. She'd gone a year without being treated like a porcelain doll, a breakable object, and she wanted life to go back to that.

"Lynn!" Amelia called.

Lynn slammed the door, drowning out whatever else her sister had been about to say. A deep shuddering sigh of relief passed through her, and she pulled her hood up to hide her face from the neighbors before starting her trek down the road.

She didn't have a destination in mind and picked one of the dirt paths that led into the woods. The thin patches of trees between their home and 'town' was the perfect place for Lynn to get her nerves under control.

She made a point of avoiding the spot in the woods where she'd heard the voices. Lynn was accustomed to six or seven regulars, but a new one, a strange one, worried her.

What if the medicine's not working anymore? she thought.

And then a new thought came. Why had the voice sounded so *sad*? The regulars came with anger or no emotion at all, but the new one was despondent.

Find me, it said.

There's no such thing as ghosts.

Looking around her town, at the decorations loudly daring any and every one to *Go to Hell,* made her less than sure. She *lived* in a ghost town. Lynn shrank in on herself when a group of tourists, a different one from the ice cream shop, appeared in her view. She made a point of going around them in a direction that took her farther from the woods.

When she'd been younger, sounds of happiness from others had been enough to cheer her up. Now, it did nothing. Part of her, deep down, couldn't deny the paranoid thought that they were laughing *at* her.

Lynn crossed the bridge ahead of her. It wasn't a real bridge of course. The structure consisted of some planked boards over a slab of concrete with large metal rings on either side, planted in the middle of the clearing with the rest of the 'town'. It was symbolic more than functional.

Running her finger along the metal loops, she studied the hundreds of locks. *Locks of Love* the bridge was called. Urban legend said if a couple added a lock to the bridge and threw the key away after crossing, they would be together forever. Lynn traced the bars, studying each one in detail. So many of the locks looked the same that it was easy to blend them together, an endless line of silver unless one really took the time to pick out the differences.

Lynn's stuck out. Not only because of the blue and red stripes across the bottom but because of what it meant to her. With shaking fingers, she held it tight, turning it slightly to see the tiny *LC + DM 4ever* etched into it. Her thumb stroked the engravings, and she held back tears as she released the lock, listening to the *clink* as it settled back into place.

Feeling eyes on her, she looked up. There, across the expanse of grass was Damien. She nearly called out when the man turned, the features shifting, and her words lodged in her throat. It wasn't him. It wasn't him, but dammit, it *looked* like him. The hazel eyes, the slope of the nose, and the long black hair.

Lynn wiped her eyes on her sleeve, hoping no one could tell how close to the edge she really was. The bridge, or the urban legend behind it, was a lie. Maybe the locks worked in a perfect world. One where both members stayed alive, but Lynn would never know.

With stiff legs, she walked the last few feet across the bridge and back into the woods. Suddenly, her sister and mother's concerns didn't seem like the worst thing that could happen to her.

Chapter Six
Jayden

IT DIDN'T TAKE long for Jayden to learn that this place really didn't have much to offer. And yet, Kasey and Kay were still somehow hard to find. Outside of the ice cream place, Jayden hid in the shadows, looking around while trying not to be seen. He pinched the bridge of his nose, ready to find his way to the hotel and leave them to their shenanigans.

Frustrated, he shoved his hands into his pockets and started to walk a line around the clearing. He did a lap, then two, before the worst of his anger began to fade. Without it, he realized he had no idea *where* he was going. There were two buildings in the distance, but for the most part, there were woods. Lots and lots of trees and undergrowth.

Jayden shivered, feeling more vulnerable than he had in a long time. He was a city boy through and through. If his car stalled and ditched him out here for the night, he might not make it until morning.

If I walk long enough, I'll either make it to my car or my friends, he told himself. Then just as quickly, *That's what the people in Blair Witch thought too.*

Jayden took two steps in the direction of the ice cream shop and froze. The girl with the black hair was there, except this time she was alone. She stood in the middle of a fake bridge, grasping one of the locks. She looked up, spotting him, and he looked away quickly.

She must think I'm an absolute creep, he thought.

As if it hadn't been enough that she'd caught him staring in the shop, now she'd caught him encroaching on a private moment of hers too.

She hurried toward him, and he thought she'd storm at him, confronting him for staring. The wind flattened her baggy hoodie to her body, and he couldn't be certain that she didn't have some sort of weapon tucked into the layers. A faraway look dotted her eyes as if she were seeing memories long gone, and when she drew close enough for him to pick up a hint of her perfume on the wind, she breezed right past him.

Jayden let out the breath he hadn't realized he'd been holding and watched her go. Something in his gut warned him he would see her again. While the thought could've been intimidating—*she* was intimidating—it comforted him.

Maybe the trip won't be so bad after all.

Chapter Seven
Lynn

WHEN LYNN WAS little, fresh air used to be enough to help her sort through the sourest mood. As she finished her walk back home, the exercise no longer provided her with relief. She thought about the man in the ice cream shop, the strange voice from the woods, her lost love, and her failed attempt at college. By the time she stood outside her house, tears threatened to leak free.

She wiped her face with the backs of her hands, trying to prepare herself to face round two of Amelia's interrogation, but she wilted. Lynn sank onto the stoop instead, burying her face in her hands. After all that had happened, she was surprised the most prominent thought was the haunting memories of Damien Moore, her lost sweetheart. Memories of him were everywhere. He was and forever would be a ghost. Everything she'd grown up with, the things she knew the best, were contaminated by his touch. Even the steps Lynn rested on held traces of him.

Lynn sniffled and wiped her nose with her knuckles, tentatively setting her fingertips on the wooden step. Her mind went back to high school, and the days they'd spend shooting the breeze, talking and joking in this very spot. When she closed her eyes, she used to be able to conjure an image of his face in perfect detail but as time passed, that ability began to fade. Everything had blurred except for his eyes. She feared that in a few more years, those would slip away as well, and the only time she'd know what he looked like would be by searching for old photographs.

The sound of his voice, however, was something she'd never be able to forget. She could still hear his laugh on cue, and she wished she had a recording of it to prove to others that it was the sweetest sound in the world. Of all the voices she'd ever heard, his was, and would always be, her favorite. She wished it would replace one of the nagging entities in her brain so they could be connected forever.

You have to let him go, Catherine's voice drifted through her mind.

Lynn closed her eyes again, not wanting to relive the ugly fight she'd had with her mother shortly before moving to Ann Arbor. Deep down, part of her knew that she would have to eventually move on, but that didn't make the process any easier. There was something comforting about the familiarity of her depression, her sorrow, and she wanted to stay there as long as she could. Leaving would mean admitting that it was all real. Admitting that she would never really see Damien again.

The front door creaked open, and she winced, holding her eyes shut to try and keep her tears to herself. If she started crying now, she wouldn't be able to stop.

"There you are," Amelia's tired voice said before she plopped down beside Lynn. Lynn could hear the worry, the fear, and that only made things worse.

"Here I am," Lynn said, hollowly, and stood on legs that felt like dead weights. She wiped her face again for extra measure and trudged her way inside, almost expecting to be ambushed by Catherine the second she stepped over the threshold.

Amelia followed, and Lynn guessed she wouldn't let her out of her sight again. At least not until they were finished playing twenty questions.

"Where did you go? I was worried," she said as Lynn hung her hoodie on the coat rack. The black against the bright floral and neon jackets from Amelia and her mother reminded Lynn of what she really was—a stain on the family. A blemish.

"Nowhere in particular," Lynn assured her, peeling off her boots. "I needed to take a walk, by myself, to regroup and refocus, you know."

"Well, you had me worried half to death," Amelia said, folding her arms across her chest. "First the blood and then you wander off? I thought you had a brain aneurysm or something."

"What can I say?" Lynn said, more exhausted than she should be as she plopped down onto the couch. "If that was the case, I wouldn't have come back, right?"

Amelia didn't look amused. She approached, standing directly between Lynn and the television on the off chance that Lynn would turn it on and use it to drown her out. "Look, I know you really hate talking about...the things that happen to you. And I'm not trying to pry or get on your nerves. I want to look out for you. That's what I've always done. Just because we're older doesn't mean I'm going to stop worrying about my baby sister."

Lynn wanted to believe that Amelia wanted the best for her, but part of her couldn't be convinced. She didn't like to be under close watch like an animal in a study. She wanted to be normal, like everyone else. If something was going to happen to her, some sort of psychotic break, she'd rather it would happen and get it over with to see if she was strong enough to pull through. The waiting and watching from Amelia, from her mother, got old quickly.

"I know," she forced herself to say at last because when she looked into Amelia's eyes, she could see no traces of a lie. "And I'm sorry. This is difficult for you, I realize, but I'm not in a good place right now. I don't want to talk about it."

Amelia pushed her lips together and slid onto the couch beside her. "I understand," she said and rested her head on Lynn's shoulder.

Normally, Lynn would've gunned it to put distance between them, but she didn't try to make an excuse this time. She stayed put, moving enough to grab the remote before settling back into the same spot. She turned the television on, leaving the first movie on that she stumbled across. It was a cheesy Hallmark Christmas movie, not something Lynn would've generally been interested in, but it was easy to lose herself in the moment with her sister.

Laughter came, and Lynn realized it had been too

long since she'd last laughed. Since she remembered that life was supposed to be occasionally enjoyed outside of the struggle of striving for a better tomorrow. Sometimes, it was important to take a break *now*.

Catherine came home not too long later with a plastic bag of groceries twisted around each of her wrists. At the sight of her daughters, she smiled a warm, genuine smile.

Lynn smiled back, thinking how good the simple action felt. Smiles invited company, and she shied away from anything that put her in the spotlight. At college, she'd feared judgment from people she let too close. People who learned the truth of how, and *what*, she really was. Instead of trying to make friends, she'd done what she could to repel people. Not smiling was a huge part of that. She'd found it easier to go about her days as a loner and had adopted a permanent scowl to keep it up.

Damien used to say you had the prettiest smile, one of the voices in her head whispered and that was all it took for the smile to fade away.

Chapter Eight
Lynn

CRICKETS STIRRED IN the night, their soft screech pulling Lynn's eyes open. The darkness overhead was broken only by soft moonlight. She stood in the woods, the soft breeze of the October night blowing through her hair. Blinking to clear away her grogginess, she did a full twirl, confused.

I already made it back home.

Lynn twitched her face, suddenly unsure. The memories had seemed so real, but that's what was so tricky about her condition. If she wasn't careful, *everything* seemed real.

Mom must be worried sick, she thought with another glance up at the moon.

Lynn shoved a handful of hair from her face and cut through the tree line. She recognized where she was: the forest always had been a place of great comfort. She and Amelia had played hide and seek out here, learning how to navigate the plants and avoid the poisonous ones. On summer nights, they'd camp out beneath the stars.

Odd how it all feels so far away now.

Lynn wrapped her arms around herself, keeping the slight chill at bay. Even when she crossed into the trees, and the moonlight didn't reach her, her steps didn't falter. She'd always prided herself on her unusual ability to see decently in the gloom. Or at least better than her sister could. The breeze blew again, ruffling the boughs of leaves overhead.

She took it all in, perfectly at peace, until the surge of voices came, punctuated with a scream.

We're here.

Come find us.

Lynn!

Heart pounding, Lynn whirled around and around, expecting a crowd of townsfolk to come staggering out of the woods, the result of another cruel prank. Somehow, the empty space in the clearing seemed even crueler, especially when the voices got louder.

"Go away!" she howled like a wounded animal and reached up to clamp her hands over her ears, desperate to block it all out.

She started to run, desperate to escape. A mottled gray hand burst from the soil, tattered fingers wrapping around her ankle. Momentum taking away her balance, she fell forward, smacking into the ground. Her screams echoed with the cacophony of noise in her brain as she kicked out, trying to free herself from her captor without taking her hands from her ears.

Part of her feared that doing so would give her brain the opportunity to explode.

"Ahh!" she screamed and kicked with all the energy she could muster until the fingers finally let go.

Lynn dragged herself a few inches away before more

hands broke through the soil, grabbing her hands and legs and pulling her to the dirt, trying to pull her down into the murkiness of the Earth. Blood poured from her ears as the hands squeezed tighter, bruising her. Dirt filled her mouth and eyes, and she caught a fleeting last glimpse of the moon before she was buried alive.

With a ragged gasp, she sat bolt upright in bed. Her eyes opened, searching for her attackers, but met her empty bedroom instead. Sunlight filtered onto the edge of her white comforter, and she stared at it, never happier to see the sun.

It was a dream, she told herself and stood on shaky legs as her door swung open.

Amelia stood in the doorframe, blonde hair pulled into a bun on top of her head. "Is everything alright?"

Lynn pushed the clinging pieces of hair off her sweaty forehead. "Yeah, just a bad dream."

"I thought that might be it. Wanna talk about it?"

Lynn shook her head. The last thing she wanted to do was *air* her crazy. "It's pretty much gone already," she lied.

Amelia stared her down, the crinkle between her eyebrows making it clear she didn't believe her, but she didn't argue. "Okay," she said and disappeared back into the hall.

As soon as she was gone, Lynn let out the breath she'd been holding. First the voices and then the nightmare?

They're trying to tell me something, she thought, shivering with foreboding.

She tried to distract herself by hurrying to the

bathroom and relieving her full bladder, but the clinging traces of the dream remained at the front of her mind. Business taken care of, she hopped in the shower, washing away the sweat in the cold water.

Feeling a bit more human, she threw on a simple outfit of jeans and a T-shirt and went downstairs for breakfast, recognizing her place. Beside her plate of eggs and bacon, her three morning pills sat in a perfect line. Lynn scowled at them as she took her seat.

"I don't have to ask which one is mine," she grumbled.

Catherine turned away from the stove, frilly pink apron fluttering. "Good morning there, Sweet Pea."

"Is it?" Lynn asked, eyeing the medication.

"It's as good as you're willing to make it," Catherine said, tossing another strip of bacon onto Lynn's plate. "Your mindset is everything."

Lynn picked up one of the strips, chewing slowly. "That's fair enough," she mused and put it down, scooping up the first pill. It was bitter and wanted to stick in her throat even with a gulp of orange juice to chase it.

"So bad dreams are back?" Catherine asked when Amelia slid into the seat beside Lynn.

Lynn forced the mouthful of juice down, cheeks burning. Amelia's eyes burned a hole in the side of her face as the silence continued.

"I don't really remember much about it," Lynn lied again and crammed the rest of her bacon strip in her mouth.

"Well, hopefully, you won't have too many more," Catherine said, eyes on the remaining medicine.

Lynn pulled her lip back into the smallest snarl and downed another pill as Catherine slung her apron onto the counter and sat in the empty seat across from Amelia and Lynn. She dipped her head, blessing the food, and Amelia joined in. Lynn hardly paused her chewing this time.

"Plans today?" Catherine asked while buttering a piece of toast.

Amelia wiped her mouth on her napkin before she said, "Kara said I could come down to the shelter today to help out, so I'm gonna do that."

"That's cool," Lynn said, perking up at the thought of not having a shadow for the day. She'd hoped to sound nonchalant, but she must've been too eager because Amelia raised one perfectly shaped eyebrow.

"You're gonna be good today, right?" Amelia prodded. "You'll take it easy?"

Lynn snorted. "You don't have to play Mom. She's right here."

Catherine waggled her fork, disapprovingly. "Oh, come now, Lynn. You know your sister worries."

"I'm going to be fine," Lynn said, catching and holding each of their gazes before she scooped up the last pill and downed it with her last sip of orange juice. She hated the way it felt going down her throat but it was a small price to pay to get her family off her back.

Breakfast done, she pushed away from the table,

scooping up her dishes to dump in the sink on her way to the front door. Amelia found her way to her side as Lynn pulled her boots on.

"Going somewhere?" she asked.

Lynn met her eyes as she grabbed her hoodie off the rack, but she didn't answer. She shrugged the familiar material on and hurried out the door, pretending she was ten years old again. She ran down the dirt road, almost expecting Amelia to run after her. Silence followed, and Lynn started to laugh.

It didn't take long for the woods to gobble up her home, and as the freedom overcame her, she ran faster and faster until her lungs strained for air. The ecstasy didn't last long before the trees reminded her of her dream, threatening to stain the rest of her day.

Nightmares weren't a thing she was used to. A period early on in her treatment, when she'd first taken her medicine, had introduced her to night terrors, but it had been such a brief experience she'd forgotten it happened.

Until now.

When Lynn closed her eyes, she could still feel the decaying hands pulling her into the dirt, the sensation of drowning on dry land.

Come find me, the voice had said.

It was the same one that had called to her from the woods.

It can't be a coincidence, she thought but immediately forced it away. If there really was something out in the woods, calling to her, what could it be? *And why me?*

Fear replaced all the good cheer she'd felt. She didn't dare take a step into the woods, instead opting to sit down on the tiny strip of cement on the side of the dirt road. She tucked her legs up to her chest, hiding her face.

Somehow, in the spiraling chaos of her brain, she remembered the worst of the worst—Damien's death.

Lynn had been at home, preparing for a pep rally at school when the phone call came. Damien had been in the woods, hunting with his brothers and cousin. It wasn't unusual. They went out every deer season, believing in eating or using every part of the animals they killed.

Lynn had never been thrilled about the idea, but she didn't chastise Damien for his interest in it. That day though, something happened. They'd gotten split up, turned around. Something had scared them, and that something had resulted in Damien's brains being blown all over the forest floor.

It was ruled an accident, but Lynn wasn't entirely convinced.

Tears prickled in Lynn's eyes, the feeling of unresolved loss eating her away. She'd never gotten the chance to say goodbye, and she never would. The trees she'd once found so much comfort in served as a home *and* prison.

Come find me, the voice danced through her head.

Lynn's tears started to harden. Could it be that maybe, just *maybe,* there was something to the voice? Something connected to Damien's death?

Chapter Nine
Lynn

O N SHAKY LEGS, Lynn stood and stumbled over to the nearest tree, brushing her fingers against the bark. She stared into the dappled shadows in the woods beyond, heart pounding.

This is a mistake, she said quickly.

There were rumors about these woods, stories about true evil, but like everything else in Hell, it could be a joke. The only way to find out for sure would be to brave it. To see for herself what the woods contained.

What if I don't come back? Lynn thought, glancing down the road in the direction of her home.

It was too easy to imagine the spectacle Catherine and Amelia would throw, the posters and rallies all in her name. The search for their *poor, sick* daughter. Most likely, they would assume the voices had been at fault, had made her wander off, and they wouldn't be wrong.

Lynn, the voice rasped, tapping into her thoughts with a jolt.

She jumped, expecting to see someone creeping through the trees. Instead, shadows greeted her.

"I can't do this," she said, taking the smallest step backward. For as much as her curiosity wanted to urge her onward, she didn't think herself brave enough. As much as she didn't want to acknowledge it, she couldn't ignore the fact that they might be right. This new voice could be an evolution of her condition, a sign that she was getting worse.

I'll let Mom take me to Dr. Phillips, she decided, turning away to begin her walk back down the highway. *That's what a proper adult would do.* Dr. Phillips would know what it meant. Might even be able to help her decode her nightmare as well.

A chaotic blast of noises flooded her mind, a surge of a thousand screams and whispers fighting to be heard over the rest. Opening her eyes to slits, she stared into the woods, tears streaking down her cheeks.

"Alright!" she screamed, not moving her hands from her ears. She ran past the first line of trees, and when the shadows engulfed her, the voices stopped.

Cautiously, Lynn lowered her hands, glancing over her shoulder toward the road before her attention went back to the path ahead.

"I'll find you," she said, softly at first but her voice grew louder with her determination. "But only because I want you to leave me alone."

She didn't know who the bargain was for, but she didn't stop to think much more about it before she continued forward. Palms itching, she wanted to bolt back toward the highway, but the thought of the voices froze her. Her ears hadn't bled from the encounter this time, but by the sick feeling it had left in her stomach, that would've been preferable.

Ducking and dodging through trees, Lynn kept her brave face on. She pulled her small pocketknife from her pocket and lashed out, using it to etch lines into the trunks of the trees as she passed.

Pressure tightened in her chest, a vice around her ribs that kept her from drawing in the air like she needed to. On each exhale, there was less room for her ribs to expand, and eventually, she could imagine it being impossible to breathe at all.

Thunder rumbled in the distance, distracting her from her internal struggle. She paused long enough to draw her hoodie around herself.

Too many red flags, she thought, and took the smallest step in the direction of the highway.

Her next breath was easier to draw in before a new voice knocked the wind from her permanently.

Lynn, don't go, it said.

"Damien?"

Lynn didn't remember the start of her run, but she weaved through the trees, heart pounding. Obstacles on the forest floor offered her little resistance as she jumped over them, going around the things too big to hop over. She didn't know where she was going, but if there was even a slight chance for her to see Damien again, she'd take the risk.

"Damien!"

Lynn pushed onward until the muscles in her thighs felt like jelly, and she feared she would collapse. For all her effort, no apparition of Damien appeared, and the other voices went silent. Thunder boomed again in the distance, and the first drop of water hit her nose as she burst through the line of trees, staring dumbfounded at the building before her.

West Gate Hospital wasn't a place many people outside of Hell knew even existed. It was secluded in its place in the woods—many of the trees had been grown for the sole purpose of keeping it hidden from view. In the 1800s, when the hospital had been fully functional, it had been a place of disposal. Somewhere to take people who were meant to disappear.

Lynn had heard stories that the hospital had held patients as young as five years old and on the other end of the spectrum, some in their 50s. It had never been made for treatment. It was a prison in disguise. Patients had been starved and tortured by the doctors. When a mysterious fire swept through it, the hospital closed its doors in the mid-20th century.

She'd expected the building to be destroyed. A burned-out husk of its former self threatening to collapse.

Lynn wrinkled her nose. The outside of the asylum looked like any other building. The grandiose towers on either side sloped to a Gothic steeple above the door. Huge bay windows decorated the bottom floor only, and Lynn guessed that was where the recreation room was. The other windows were small and barred, tiny little things lined up perfectly within the crumbling brick walls.

A strike of lightning crashed to the ground not ten

feet away, singeing the grass black where it struck. Lynn choked on her air, instantly dizzy. If it had hit any closer, it would've killed her, and no one would know where she was.

Lynn glanced back to the building again, shaking all over as she broke herself from the trance.

Damien's dead, she told herself the cruel ugly truth she didn't want to accept.

She'd end up the same way if she kept giving into her brain, letting it take her to places she knew were no good for her. Lynn was ready to wave off the entire adventure when the ground beneath her started to shake, the sky overhead turning an unsightly orange. Lynn had never been through a lot of natural disasters, but she knew danger when it came knocking.

The trees around her pulled and whipped violently in the heavy wind, and then she could hear it—a tornado. Lynn screeched. Going back toward the highway would lead her right into its path. Without any other option, she ran toward the asylum, the only shelter in sight, and flung the doors open.

Chapter Ten
Jayden

JAYDEN HADN'T BEEN able to find Kay and Kasey. After a two hour frustrating search, there was nothing left for him to do but give up. He got in his car and made his way to the motel only to see Kasey's vehicle already parked outside.

Of course, he thought as he stared at the familiar license plate. What better way to deflate a third wheel than to ditch him?

I need new friends, he thought and trudged into the building.

The smell of stiff cleaners rose up as soon as he opened the door to his room. Jayden threw his bag on the counter and jumped into bed. It didn't take much effort for him to fall asleep. When he woke in the morning, he had a missed page.

Hey, what happened, man? Couldn't find you last night.

Jayden screwed his face up, imagining what he would say.

As if it wasn't bad enough they'd decided to ditch him, but gaslighting him about it on top of it was the icing on the cake. Jayden groaned in his throat and threw his pager across the bed. He'd have a serious talk with Kasey soon, but not now. Not when he was still this angry. He'd only trip on his emotions, and that wouldn't help anyone.

To distract himself, he scooped up the remote to the television and turned it on. The first channel that came to life uninfected by static was a news broadcast playing the weather. The man warned of rain which could turn into a full-on storm. A tornado.

At least they didn't make me play hide-and-seek today, Jayden thought.

As if on cue, the phone to his room started to ring. He could guess who it was but found himself reaching for it to hang it up. Petty? Yes, but he couldn't help it. He'd never abandon his friends in such a way and hated that they didn't think of him in the same manner.

Do they even consider me to be their friend? he found himself wondering.

Jayden relaxed back onto the bed, lacing his fingers together behind his head. The weatherman's droning voice made him drowsy, and he closed his eyes, considering going back to sleep. Kasey could wait on *him* this time.

When he opened his eyes again, he was still in the room, on his bed. With a grunt, he sat up and put his fingers to the pain in the side of his neck. He scooped up the remote, ready to turn off the television and call a truce with Kasey.

"You need to go back," the weatherman said.

Jayden blinked and squinted, certain he was hearing things. "Huh?"

The weatherman turned in Jayden's direction, an

unsettling smile spreading across his face. "They need you," he said. "*She* needs you."

"Who does?" he asked, heart pounding.

Jayden blinked, and when he opened his eyes again, the weatherman was gone, replaced by the news anchor at the front desk. Still shaking with the aftereffects of the dream, Jayden grabbed his pager to see three more calls from Kasey. He rose from the bed and stretched when he dialed Kasey's number rang and rang and rang.

His friend didn't answer, and Jayden wouldn't be surprised if he'd decided to give Jayden a taste of his own medicine.

He wouldn't do that, Jayden told himself. It was easy to believe with the feeling deep in his gut, the one that warned him that something was wrong.

Chapter Eleven

Lynn

LYNN DIDN'T KNOW what she expected the inside of the asylum to look like. She'd seen a lot of scary movies with dingy dwellings and burned-out husks of buildings. She expected it to look something like that, except when the orange light of the evening poured in, she could see enough to tell that the inside of the hospital was undamaged.

Was this really West Gate? Or had another asylum sprung up here? *Or maybe the fire never happened.*

Lynn shivered with uncertainty.

Some mysteries are better left unsolved, she decided and turned to look outside, not letting go of the door.

Before she could take a step outside, the sky erupted in a waterfall of rain that hit the ground with such force the drops bounced back up a second time. The grass around the hospital turned to a thick mud bed within a few minutes.

So much for that, Lynn thought, remembering how close the lightning had already come to hitting her. If it hit any of the water as she crossed through, she'd be doomed.

Lynn rolled her bottom lip in her teeth and watched the rain. On a good day, it brought her comfort, the sound washing away the unease and stress that built up the rest of the time.

The storm won't last forever, she told herself. She

could wait it out. At least until the storm moved farther away.

You can do that, one of her regular voices taunted her. *If you want to die here.*

Lynn frowned, digging into her pockets. The little orange bottle wasn't there. A tiny jolt of fear pierced through her, and she patted harder, checking every pocket in turn.

It must've fallen out when I was running, she realized, and that brought an entirely new level of fear. She had no phone, no way to let anyone know where she was, and now, she also didn't have her meds to tide her over.

Amelia is never going to let me hear the end of this.

You're going to die here, a voice chimed up, but it wasn't her regular. It was the tinny one, the one that had called to her from the road.

Except it wasn't in her head this time. Someone whispered it right in her ear. Screaming, she stumbled away from the door, losing contact in her desperate attempt to keep herself righted. It slammed shut, submerging her in the dim pit of the hospital. She rushed to pull the door back open, but it wouldn't budge. She pulled with all the strength in her, but the hinges, which had been perfect a minute ago, were now rusted over, keeping the door shut. Lynn leaned closer, wondering if she was mistaken. She reached out, running her finger over the jagged edges. Not even a crack of light got through. She'd have to find a different way out, an emergency exit or passageway.

There's no way out, a voice taunted her. She didn't

want to feed into it, to give it strength, but it was hard when she remembered that this place had been *built* as a prison. It hadn't been created to make escape easy.

You'll never get out by standing there, one of her regular voices jeered.

Lynn sometimes had the powerful urge to scowl at them, and she hated that none of them had a face, or eyes, she could stare into. She'd imagined what they might look like, but it didn't satisfy that desire.

Putting on a brave face, she started to walk down the hall. It was dark, and with nighttime approaching, it would only get worse. If she wandered too deep into the building, it might be too dark for her to find her way out again.

Lynn bayed in the middle of the hall, faltering between waiting by the doors in the slim chance someone would open it in a desperate attempt to seek shelter from the storm. Or looking for an exit.

No one else is foolish enough to come all the way out here, she thought and buried her face in her hands. She slunk to the floor, unable to bring herself to move. She could've stayed like that for hours, but then a scream rang out, louder and more violent as it echoed down the empty corridor.

Chapter Twelve

Jayden

JAYDEN DROVE QUICKLY, foot pressing the pedal all the way to the floor as he rushed down the highway. Unkind thoughts swirled in his head, mixed with his dream. The lack of response from Kasey the most troubling part of all. He dialed his friend again before leaving but received no answer.

Why isn't he picking up?

Every time Jayden blinked, he saw the creepy weatherman's eerie smile. *They need you. She needs you.*

"It's a coincidence," Jayden told himself out loud.

Reaching for the radio, he thought a song might help calm his racing heart. A lot of static came through instead. He flicked up and down, but most of the stations were blocked by the ring of trees on either side of the road.

A static version of *The Ring of Fire* didn't ease his anxiety at all. He hurried to shut off the station. In the oncoming night, it was hard to tell exactly where the tiny town started. He increased the speed of his wiper blades, but it didn't make it much easier to see. He would've driven right through town if a car didn't emerge, blocking his path.

Desperate to avoid impact, he slammed his foot on the brake. The backend fishtailed and spun, thrusting Jayden forward until the car crashed into the railing on the side of the road. Jayden's head slammed into the steering wheel, the airbag activating a second too late. Winded, he blinked and sat up, a line of blood trickling from a gash above his eye.

Jayden breathed in, ragged air getting stuck in his throat. Beyond the shattered windshield rose the twisted pieces of the front of his car, smoke rising from the engine. His car was totaled. Shaking, Jayden looked at his hands. Somehow, he wasn't badly hurt.

With shaking fingers, he hurried to undo his belt, throwing himself out of the car and onto the road. The pebbles ripped open his flesh, dirt seeping into the wounds. He ground his teeth but hopped to his feet. Half out of his mind with adrenaline and fear, Jayden stumbled across the road. The other car stayed sideways across both lanes of the highway.

Jayden wiped the water from his eyes and got closer. A sickening feeling of familiarity washed through him.

"What the hell?" Jayden said and approached the driver's door, whipping it open.

There was no one inside. No clue anyone had been in the car for a while. Jayden patted down the seats and around the steering wheel but didn't find the keys. He scratched his head and backed out of the car, standing beside it, dumbfounded.

Where *was* Kasey? Or Kay even.

Cursing, Jayden paced back and forth, raking his hands through his hair. Something had happened to his friends. He might've been able to convince himself otherwise in the hotel room but standing before the evidence made him sick. Kasey had worked too hard to get this car. He might have a habit of ditching his friends, but his car?

Never.

Jayden glanced up and down the path. There was nothing but shadows and forest for miles. The odds of someone happening down this way to help him were slim to none. He wiped the blood from his forehead and did another check of himself for damage. He seemed to be okay from the wreck, but he could have a concussion he wasn't yet aware of. What happened if he wandered off and passed out?

"Fuck!" he screamed at the top of his lungs.

A nearby owl hooted in response, and Jayden jumped, turning in the direction of the noise. There was no telling what other creatures' attention he might've drawn. With the scent of his blood in the air, he didn't want to take any chances. He went back to Kasey's car, searching through the backseat on the off chance the keys somehow made it back there.

Nothing.

This way, a voice hissed, words so crisp they could've been spoken directly in his ear.

He shot out of the car so fast he nearly avoided banging his head on the roof of his friend's car. Glancing over his shoulder, he saw nothing in the rain and did a complete twirl, certain he had heard...*someone.*

I'm here, the voice said again, pulling his attention to the woods.

No light made it to the ground, and the rain had washed away any possibility of a trail, making Jayden unsure if Kasey had gone this way or not.

He'd never do that, Jayden told himself.

They need you.

The same voice from his dreams called to him. Through unknown forces, he found himself walking across the pavement and past the first line of trees.

Chapter Thirteen
Lynn

WHEN LYNN FINALLY picked herself up, she went to the door, double-checking to see if the rusted hinges had magically unrusted themselves. When she found that they had not, she pressed her back to the wall, staring down the dingy corridor with the echo of the scream ringing in her ears.

"Hello?" she called in a voice that came out so shaky she was nearly breathless.

Another scream echoed back in response, this one weaker than before. Lynn held her hands over her ears, closing her eyes to block it all out. She hadn't ruled out the possibility that it was all in her head. An illusion created from her fear. When nothing appeared from the shadows, she only became more convinced.

Lynn reached into her pocket, grateful that at least her knife was still there. She pulled it out, brandishing it before her. She took a step forward, faltered, and frowned. Her entire life she'd been passive, letting things happen, letting people treat her as they would. The end result? Her life had taken her in a complete circle.

Lynn liked to believe that hard times taught lessons. Maybe the point of this entire adventure was to teach her to grow a backbone, to come out of her shell.

Or it's to get you murdered, one of her regular voices said.

Lynn narrowed her eyes to slits. *Shut up,* she told it, oddly glad for the anger it inspired.

Rage leading her by the hand, she walked down the corridor. With her free hand, she pressed her fingertips to the walls, feeling the old paint and lines in the bricks. Old feces and rot filled her nose, and she scrunched her face, wondering if she'd stumble across any dead animals.

Crash.

Something metal and hard jabbed into the wall at the end of the hall followed by a high-pitched scream. Instead of choking off like the previous one had, it ended in a garbled *"Please"*, before dying away.

Someone's hurt, she realized.

A whirlwind of emotions swept over her at the thought that she *wasn't* alone in here. That someone else had stumbled across the asylum first. Lynn moved faster, on the verge of a jog. A dangerous move considering her foot could catch on debris or she could cut herself on something rusty.

I can't waste time, she convinced herself.

Whoever it was, they were getting weaker. Lynn's heartbeat pounded in time with her footsteps as she turned the corner, skidding to a halt. If she'd thought the previous hallway was hard to see, it had nothing on this one. Lynn was reminded of an underground cavern.

Some of those caves had horrible creatures in them, a voice sneered.

Lynn shivered, taking the smallest step forward before she called in a shaky voice, "Can you hear me?"

The *thud* of a heavy piece of furniture moving in one of the nearby rooms came out, and Lynn felt sick all over again. What if the sound she'd heard earlier had been a trap? A lure to get her caught off guard so someone could sneak up behind her and rob her? Or worse?

Lynn did a three-sixty with the knife clasped between both her hands. "Show yourself!"

A deep, guttural scream came from the hallway *behind* her, the one she'd left. Lynn had barely been prepared for an encounter with a human let alone whatever was capable of making such a sound. In her state of panic, she couldn't put an image to it, and the fear of the unknown made her bolt. She ran down the hallway, slamming into a set of double doors that swung open upon impact.

The recreation room stretched ahead of her. The difference here? She could *see*. A patch of the ceiling had rotted away, allowing rain and moonlight to stream inside. Lynn barely avoided slipping in the puddles of water as she hurried through. Heavy footsteps on the other side of the door let her know that whatever had been chasing her, hadn't lost interest.

Panicked, she ducked around the rotted couch, skidding to a halt. The room used to be white. She could tell that in the splotches on the walls that *weren't* covered in pools of sticky liquid. Sickly sweet copper drifted up her nose, and Lynn stumbled backward, trying to get out of the room. Her foot hit something solid, and she bent down to get closer to it.

Reaching out one shaky finger, she poked it and recoiled. It was squishy, like flesh. Her eyes traveled the length of the object, and she threw herself backward. It was an *arm*. A *human* arm. Lynn backed herself against the wall, breaths coming faster and faster until she was so lightheaded the entire world spun.

The thing that did this has you in its sights, one of her voices warned.

Lynn couldn't stop shaking. In the shadows, it was hard to tell much about the rest of the body. It was small and slender, feminine. Sniffling, she tried to feel for a pulse and her hand came away covered in blood. She couldn't hear any sounds of breathing, and that was enough. She didn't want to see what was left. Her hand pressed to her mouth to stifle her cries, she tried to come up with a plan, but couldn't get rid of a clinging thought: whoever this had been, she's been dead for a while.

So where did the screams come from?

Chapter Fourteen
Jayden

JAYDEN VOWED TO only go a short distance into the woods and come right back out. Between the blackness and his head wound, he didn't trust himself to not get lost.

"Kasey!" he screamed, moving as quickly as he could without actually sprinting. It'd be his luck he'd run headfirst into a tree and do what the wreck had not.

Green leaves sagged under the weight of the rain, the woods more unwelcoming than they'd appeared during the day. Nothing seemed out of place, but Jayden thought of *the Blair Witch Project* and the way the actors had run needlessly through the woods to their death.

He wanted to tell himself it was all ridiculous, but *something* had happened to his friends. And he was the only one who knew.

So Jayden kept going, rain soaking him through to the skin until he knew he risked sickness as well as getting lost. He would've turned around, except it was already too late. He couldn't discern which direction would take him back to the road.

I should've joined the boy scouts, he thought, remembering a long-lost argument he'd had with his parents. Why had he been so against the idea?

Jayden looked left and right, coming to the

realization that he might have to seek shelter to ride out the storm. Defeated, he sunk to the ground, ignoring the feeling of cold mud sinking through his pants to his skin.

This way, a tiny voice lilted.

Jayden's head snapped up with such ferocity a tiny spasm of pain blossomed in his neck. Wincing, he pressed his fingers to the spot and sought out the person who must be hiding nearby.

"Hello?" he called.

Pounding rain greeted him. Uneasy, Jayden rose to his feet, convinced he was losing his mind. It was the second time he'd heard that voice, third if counted the *dream* in his hotel room. Except now, he wasn't so sure it had been a dream. If someone was following him, he would've seen some sign of that...right?

Whatever it is, Kasey must've heard it too, Jayden thought, thinking again of his friend's eerily empty car. It made sense. Kasey always drove with the window down. If someone called for help, he would've been the first to try and find them, not realizing he was the only one in danger.

"Who are you?" Jayden demanded, clenching his hands into fists.

Against a person, he was sure he could fight his way back to safety. Against the unknown, his confidence wavered. He patted his pockets in search of a weapon he knew he didn't have. He had a lighter in his back pocket, but the rain had most likely made sure it was worthless.

Thunder boomed, the sound shaking his bones, and a

shock of lightning cut through the gray, coming to the Earth closer than he'd ever seen lightning come before. The trees blocked its final landing place, and Jayden was grateful for the coverage. As soaked as he was, he feared he'd make the perfect lightning rod.

Teeth chattering, Jayden scurried into the nearby undergrowth in search of shelter. Under the wide leaves, the rain didn't have such easy access to him, but he was cold. He sunk to the ground, curling himself into a ball to hold onto what bit of warmth he could. He blinked and when his eyes re-opened, the storm has passed.

Watery sunlight dappled the ground around him, and Jayden audibly gasped. He lifted his shaking hands, turning them over to study the palms that weren't his. Closer inspection showed his clothes were gone too. He was cloaked in a camouflage jacket and pants he didn't recognize. Definitely not his style.

"Coming or what?" a guy with a long blond ponytail called. The sunlight made a mole on the edge of his cheekbone stand out.

Jayden blinked, unable to decide which part of his situation was the biggest shock. The change in time of day, the appearance of these men, or the fact that he seemed to be *taller?*

Who is this man? he wondered and opened his mouth to ask.

Different words poured out instead. "Always so damn impatient," he said and rolled his eyes, but he didn't understand why.

He felt like a giant marionette, a puppet whose strings were pulled by some invisible figure. Under this spell, he started to walk, and the blond man laughed, tossing a firearm into Jayden's hands. He nearly buckled under the weight, panicking about the exact places to put his hands. He'd never held anything closer to a gun than a water gun.

The person whose body he seemed to have taken over didn't share his hesitation. He grabbed the shotgun with practiced ease, hoisting it up so that the barrel rested against his shoulder to point at the sky. Jayden tried to turn his head, to get a better view of his surroundings, but found he couldn't control much more than blink on occasion.

He became aware of the presence of a third member of the group as they traveled. Another man, this one close to Jayden's age with deep-set eyes and short brown hair. He had a shotgun too, but his was lifted so that the barrel pointed at the back of the blond's head.

Jayden wanted to scream, to call a warning when he realized the other man was joking. He snorted and shot a grin to Jayden that Jayden could feel his face return though he didn't get it. He tried again to open his mouth, to ask these people who they were and what was going on. Instead, he continued to walk with them, keeping all his questions to himself.

"How much farther 'til the stand?" the brunette beside Jayden asked.

The blond glanced over his shoulder. "Not much

longer," he said, holding his eyes closed as if he were growing frustrated with the entire situation. "God, you guys complain so friggin' much you'd think you didn't want to be here."

He turned back around, leading the way, and the man beside Jayden fidgeted with his gun again, mock shooting the blond once more. Jayden laughed, this time in on the joke, and when the blond looked over his shoulder, Jayden pretended he hadn't made a sound.

"Clearing's up ahead," he said, pushing through a break in the trees and undergrowth.

Jayden picked up his feet, careful to not trip on himself. Enraptured in his footsteps, he hadn't realized the blond stopped walking until Jayden nearly crashed into him.

"Well, that's not it," the sullen brown-haired man said.

"No shit," the blond sniped and elbowed Jayden. "Hey, you know what this place is, right?"

Jayden was relieved when his head shook back and forth. Whoever this person was, they were as clueless as he was.

"West Gate Hospital. According to urban legend, this place was abandoned years ago after like a shit ton of mental people died."

"Shouldn't call 'em that, man," the brown-haired man said. "It was an insane asylum. They weren't *killed* here."

The blond shrugged. "Depends on who you listen to. I mean, everyone who was brought here, disappeared. No one knows where they went. You know how you make someone disappear forever? You *kill* them."

"Whatever. It's all a stupid legend anyway."

"Is it?" the blond tipped his head to the side. "Last I checked, legends don't leave buildings behind."

"This place could've been anything. You know how people around here love their drama. For all we know this is an old factory or something."

"If you don't believe me, look it up," the blond said, not sounding put out. "Prove me wrong."

"You're on."

Jayden didn't know what to think of the argument. When he and Kasey had started planning their trip to Hell, they'd done plenty of research on the town and the area surrounding it. Nothing had come up about an asylum, and he had to wonder if the brown-haired man was right about it being an urban legend.

If it was real, it wouldn't be advertised, he reminded himself.

It wouldn't be safe for curious people who decided to poke around.

I don't know what is *real anymore,* he thought when he considered the fact that he was living in someone's memories and had no idea whose they were and how he could escape. None of the voices sounded like the one that had lured him into the woods, but being inside this person's head made it hard to decide. The voice that came out sounded like his own.

I'm crazy. I'm officially crazy.

The group crept back into the woods, edging around the clearing with the looming, crumbling building. Just as soon as they'd started, they stopped again, the blond holding up a hand for added effect. "You guys hear that?"

Jayden didn't hear anything and looked at the other men's faces to try to gauge what was happening.

"Shit, you think it's a bear?"

"Hell if I know, but I'm not going to stand around and find out," the blond said and took off running through the trees.

Jayden and the other man were a moment behind. Jayden, being shorter than both of them, quickly fell behind until the other men disappeared into the foliage ahead. Relying on his hearing, he tried to follow.

The fear in Jayden's mind and the person whose body he had inhabited were at the same level. He tried to take another glance over his shoulder, to gauge how much longer he had to live, and his foot caught in a root. Unable to catch himself, he tumbled to the ground.

The foliage behind him exploded, and Jayden screamed. It wasn't a bear that appeared or any other such beast. Instead, a man crept toward him. His eyes were two deep pits of blackness perched above a smile so red it looked as if blood seeped from the gaps between his teeth. Jayden had no awareness of himself until a blood-curdling scream fell from his lips.

The creature lunged toward him, ghostly hands

encircling him before he could move. The thing came closer and closer until Jayden imagined it would suck his soul right out of his body. He felt sick. Not like himself.

Then everything in him drained away, and a predator took over. The footsteps of his fleeing companions were loud, the smell of their sweat prominent. Jayden started to move toward them.

Something's wrong, he thought and tried to back out. To pull away, but he had the horrific sensation of no longer having control over his body.

He was *hunting.*

He ran and ran, catching glimpses of moving camouflage outfits through the trees. A guttural roar sounded, and Jayden cried out, certain that whatever it was would get him when the sound came again, and he realized it came *from* him.

One gunshot rang out, blackening Jayden's peripheral vision. Another gunshot sounded far away, and the world cut to black.

Chapter Fifteen
Lynn

LYNN HELD HER breath, almost wishing she would pass out so that fate would take over, and she wouldn't be responsible for handling the next, possibly last, moments of her life. She searched for a hiding place that didn't exist in the wide, airy room as the creature grew ever closer. With the echo of its roar, it was hard to tell exactly how close the creature was, but before it burst into the room, the sound stopped.

Lynn drew her eyebrows together, staring at the door, confused. *Am I already dead?*

Had it been so quick that she had no memory of it happening? Lynn patted herself down, feeling as real as she ever had.

Could it be that whatever was following her decided to wait for her to let her guard down and would lunge when she opened the door? Lynn carefully picked her way across the room, setting her hand on the dingy wall beside the doors. She pressed her ear to the wood, listening, convinced she'd hear stirring or breathing. Some sign she was right.

She heard neither.

Lynn took a tiny half step backward, nearly slipping in a puddle of blood. It could've been easy enough to believe all the sounds had been the result of her condition if not for *this.* There was *something* else stalking the building, and it had her scent.

So where is it now? one of the voices asked.

She didn't know.

The more she thought about her situation, the less she was sure of anything. *Everything* could be a byproduct of her delusional mind. Sniffling, Lynn crouched down, dragging her fingers through the blood. It was cold and sticky. She lifted her fingers to her face and sniffed, the iron tang filling her nose.

Lynn jumped up and wiped the blood on her pants. She wasn't imagining this—the sights, smells, the *feel* on her skin. It was all real, and that meant she was very much in danger.

This way, a tiny voice cooed.

Lynn went ramrod straight. It was the voice she'd first heard by the road. The one that had led her into this mess.

Lynn did a circle, hoping to see *someone* responsible lurking in the nearest shadows. Nothing looked back at her. Lynn backed away from the blood puddle, standing in the perfect center of the room. From that angle, she spotted the wide window she'd seen from the outside. A bit of moonlight filtered in through the bars. Soft pattering told her the rain continued to rage on outside.

What do I do? she thought, beginning to feel crazy for a new reason.

She couldn't stay there, yet, the idea of traveling

back into the hallway made her freeze. She didn't know where the creature had gone or if it would make its rounds back through.

You don't want to be here when it comes back, one of her voices warned.

She couldn't deny that. So, she crept toward the door, fingertips brushing the wall. Before she hit the exit, something grasped her ankle, and she halted, nearly falling forward from the unexpected force. She screamed before she could stop herself and hurried to cover her mouth, looking down to see what had grabbed her.

Partly, she expected to see a grotesque hand trying to drag her to Hell like her nightmare. Nothing. She kicked out and her toes met the brick wall. Whatever had grabbed her, had vanished.

I'm losing my mind, she thought and crouched down, patting her ankle.

When she looked up, a beam of moonlight glinted off something silver mounted near the ceiling. An air vent. Lynn's eyes went wide, and she ducked closer. Curiously, she grabbed the grate cover by the edges and pulled, removing it with ease. It hadn't been screwed in, and Lynn wondered if other people had used it to escape. Could there have been another person here when the other one was killed?

Lynn peered into the hole, trying to gauge which direction it went. She didn't know if it would lead her outside or deeper into the building, but she'd take her chances. Tiny spaces usually sent her into a spiral, but she crawled inside, surprised that there was enough space for her to maneuver and breathe without the feeling the walls would crush her. She pressed herself against the wall, angling her arm to scoop the grate up and prop it up over the hole, hoping it would be enough to keep her safe in the off chance the creature would return for her.

Chapter Sixteen
Jayden

JAYDEN'S EYES SHOT open, and he gasped for air. A blossom of pain roared in his chest as if he'd actually been shot. He touched the spot, relieved there was no wound. The relief was short lived when his surroundings came back to him. He lay in the mud on the forest floor, rain pouring down on him. Coughing, he sat up, shivering violently. He hugged himself for warmth, but only succeeded in squeezing some of the water out of his clothes and made himself colder.

Squinting, he thought the trees around him had thinned, but he couldn't be sure. Everything had been so hazy before the vision had overtaken him. What *had* that been? A result of his head wound or something more?

Who were those people? And why had they chosen *him*?

Delirious, Jayden took a step forward, and then another. Looming before him sat a massive white building. The same one from his vision. *West Gate Hospital* as the blond had called it. From the outside, it looked unwelcoming, and he couldn't imagine anything worse than going inside. Overhead, the rain continued. If he stayed outside, he'd only get colder.

He would've thrown himself under an overpass if it meant shielding himself from the weather. Teeth chattering, he hurried through the large black gate. The faint hint of ash lingered in the back of his nostrils as he circled the building past barred windows. With squishing steps, he rounded the corner and hurried up the overgrown path to the door, fingers slipping across the handle. He pulled, relieved when it opened with relative ease.

Jayden stepped inside, breathing in the dusty air. A light breeze brushed his wet skin, and he hugged himself tighter, wondering if he'd be able to find a towel or an abandoned set of clothes. Before the door swung closed behind him, a streak of lightning tore across the sky, and he guessed the storm wouldn't be over any time soon.

The door closed, immersing him in darkness. A few faint beams of light streamed in under the door, but it was barely enough to see. If Kasey had found his way here, he could be anywhere. Jayden ruffled his wet hair and wrang the extra water out of his clothes, considering stripping off his hoodie and shirt. The idea left him feeling vulnerable.

He pushed the door, wanting to leave it propped open for whatever bit of light it could provide. It didn't budge. Heart rate increasing, Jayden rammed his shoulder into it, straining under its solidity but made no progress.

"Son of a bitch!"

Puffing his cheeks, Jayden closed his eyes and tried to picture the building as he'd seen it from outside. He couldn't remember seeing another door, but surely, there had to be one, right?

"Everyone who was brought here disappeared. No

one knows where they went. You know how you make someone disappear forever? You kill them," the blond's words echoed in his head again.

Just like that, he was angry—angry at Kasey for planning this trip, angry at Kay for causing the rift in his friend's interest, angry at himself for getting lost in the woods, and most importantly, angry at whatever force had led him here.

There has to be some purpose, he thought because he refused to believe he'd been led to this place solely to die.

Chapter Seventeen
Lynn

WHEN LYNN HAD convinced herself to squeeze into the vent, it had been with the assumption it would only be a brief journey until she could find a way out. How wrong she'd been.

The vent went on longer and longer, and Lynn started to hallucinate that it was a direct portal to Hell. That she would be trapped forever in the shadowy claustrophobic results of her own bad decisions. She turned a corner, and the path shrunk, the metal edges grazing the edges of her shoulders and leaving her with the worry it would eventually be so small she'd get stuck. It didn't, but the fear lingered.

Beneath her, a slit in the metal grating allowed her a peek into the room below. She could see nothing but blackness. Several times, she passed similar views. Vaguely, she was comforted by the thought of escape but pondering what could be lurking in those thick ugly shadows kept her hiding.

Lynn hadn't seen the beast responsible for the noises in the hallway. Her brain improvised and created its own creature with lots of tentacles, teeth, and claws. A chill raced down her spine, and she forced herself to keep moving, slightly faster. Her hand touched down on another grate. As soon as she put her weight into it, it gave out. Without anything to hold onto, she fell, landing on the hard ground with a splat.

Groaning, she got up on her knees, patting down the points of impact on her ribs and hips to help ease away the worst of the pain. She blinked, and the room brightened with a different kind of light. Lynn's heart hammered in her chest, except it *wasn't* her chest. She tried to move and found her body wouldn't obey. It dashed forward, footsteps echoing around the room.

Something behind her crashed. It was loud, so loud she could hardly tell if it was in the same room as her or the next room over. The girl didn't stop running. Her breathing grew louder, filling with exertion, but her eyes trained on the closet ahead of her. She jumped inside, slamming it closed. The space was cramped, filled with medical equipment that ranged from needles to gauze, to a variety of other things.

The woman didn't pay attention to any of it. Her hands were locked on the doorknob, holding the door closed the best she could. She peered through the tiny gap that remained, heart thrumming. Lynn blinked, wondering if she would see the monster that had chased her.

Nothing appeared.

Lynn had the sickening thought that she was trapped inside someone who had a worse mental condition than she did.

Then a man appeared.

He was tall and muscular, cloaked in the white apparel of a 19th century doctor. A white cloth mask hid half his face, and he swiveled his head back and forth, curly black hair moving with him. Lynn raised a hand to cover her mouth, barely resisting the urge to cry. The fear blossoming deep in the woman's stomach was so primal, so raw, Lynn could hardly process it.

Even when her mind had started to deteriorate, she'd never felt so afraid.

The man moved with a swiftness that seemed inhumane. He flung the doors open with such ferocity, that Lynn screamed and threw herself backward. When she opened her eyes, she realized she was back in her own body. Shaking, she looked left and right, convinced the man would appear from the shadows and get her.

What happened? she asked herself over and over.

She held a hand over her heart, wishing to hear the taunting mockery of one of her voices. For them to confirm that this was all in her head, and she was on a steep decline into insanity. Lynn waited, but for once, the voices in her head were silent.

Chapter Eighteen
Jayden

JAYDEN SPENT LONGER than he dared to admit baying at the entrance of the hospital and telling himself how stupid he was to be afraid. The biggest threat the building most likely had were rats and spiders, both of which were things he'd stopped fearing years ago.

If Kasey had passed through this way, he wouldn't stand in place, waiting on rescue. He'd be on the move.

Jayden needed to be too. "Kasey?"

Soft scampering pattered across the floor near the wall, and Jayden wrinkled his nose. There definitely *were* rats here, but Jayden wasn't surprised. Step by step, Jayden walked through the lobby, studying everything around.

It was empty save for a busted chair lying on its side in the corner. Jayden walked through the room, emerging on the hall on the other side. Remains of hospital beds, rusty equipment, and ash littered the hall.

The blond wasn't lying about the fire.

Remembering the flashback reminded him of the other things that had been said. If people really came here to die, would there still be evidence of it?

Fire destroys everything, he thought, not quite sure why he was so rattled by the fact.

If people had died here, it had happened so long in

the past that the stories had passed the point of being cold case files and had entered legend status. He couldn't change anything by solving them. The only thing he could save at this point was himself. Jayden frowned, still painfully aware that the seemingly only door had stuck shut.

That's why I need to find another exit.

He chanted his goal in his head over and over again, a mantra to keep him focused on his goal. Everything else could be put on the back burner until he achieved that much.

Dragging one soggy foot after the other, he made his way down the hall. Logically, he knew he was alone, but after a while, he didn't feel he was. An unsettling chill down the length of his spine warned him he was being watched. Something about the gloom, the thought of not being able to *be* seen called to him. Before he knew it, he became part of the shadows, setting his fingers to the wall to serve as a guide onward.

He kept his ears on high alert, listening for sounds of life. *Any* signs that weren't rodent-related of course. The only thing he registered was his own heartbeat so he focused on what his other senses could tell him. The air was musty and ashy, starlight trickling in from a hole in the ceiling. Jayden stared up at it, contemplating the possibility of using it as a way to get out when he heard a crash from down the hall.

On instinct, he ducked, hoping to not be seen. Blood thundering in his ears, Jayden debated his next move—keep his distance or investigate. How many times had he screamed at the characters in movies for making a decision like that?

A smart person would run screaming in the opposite direction.

It could be Kasey.

Against his every instinct, he crept onward, sticking to the shadows as much as possible. He lingered outside the entrance of the room and listened. The sounds had stopped, but he was positive this was where they had come from. He mustered enough courage to peek inside. Moonlight drifted through the bars on the window, but it wasn't enough to chase away the shadows from every corner. Jayden squinted, but it didn't make it easier to see. He couldn't tell if anyone was there or *had* been there.

Something compelled him to move inside, and he followed the urge, but something felt off. A presence he couldn't quite put his finger on. The smell was different here too. The lingering smell of ash was accompanied by something else.

Something metallic.

Jayden recognized the new smell before he stepped on something solid. It rolled beneath him, and he'd been so caught off guard that he lost his balance. Slamming to the floor with a groan, pain shot up his elbow and his hip. Blood filled his mouth from where he'd bitten his tongue. Swallowing it down, he narrowed his eyes to try and better see what he'd fallen over.

It was smooth and cylindrical. Jayden blinked and tried to better clear his vision. It couldn't be what it looked like. It couldn't be an arm.

It's a mannequin, he told himself for lack of a better explanation and reached out to touch it.

Soft flesh squished beneath his fingertip. Repulsed, he threw up, stomach acid adding to the horrible smell in the room. Jayden looked from it to the arm. He traced it up to the small form of a girl and threw up again, breaking into a series of retches that made his entire abdomen hurt. When the dry heaves stopped, he screamed loud and long forgetting that he was trying to make himself small and quiet. Forgetting the possible dangers that could be lurking nearby.

He screamed with everything in him, hoping it would be enough for people to hear from the road.

Chapter Nineteen

Lynn

LYNN HAD NEVER heard a more terrified scream in her entire life. The sound was so loud, so sudden, that she ducked back into the closet without thinking about it. There *was* someone else in here. Someone who *hadn't* been killed by the awful creature that lurked in its depths.

Another person could make things better. She wanted to run to him. It was human nature to not want to be alone, and after all she'd seen, even a dangerous thief seemed like better company than her own.

A broken metal pipe lay on the ground outside of the closet, and Lynn scooped it up, clutching it tightly in both hands before she looked around the room, searching for a way out. A door lay across the room, but it was held in place by a pile of rubble. Lynn guessed the room beyond had collapsed from the fire. Cursing, she looked back up at the vent.

From what she could tell, it was the only way in or out of the room. She couldn't see the opening, and standing on her tiptoes didn't give her the height to reach it. Neither did a few loose pieces of tile she managed to pry up. Lynn turned her attention to the rubble blocking the door and sought out the largest block of concrete she could move.

Straining under its weight, she dragged it, the sound

louder in her head than it probably was in reality. Kicking the other pieces out of the way, Lynn positioned it under the hole. Nudging it with her toe to test its stability, she determined it wouldn't slide...easily at least.

Move slow and steady.

Lynn balanced on it, using the wall to keep her steady as she stood on her tiptoes, reaching up with one hand. She waved left and right, panic beginning to eat at her when her hand finally touched the edge of the opening. Breathing out, she took her other hand off the wall and curled her fingers around the edges of the vent. She tossed the pipe up first before heaving herself up.

At first, she dangled helplessly. She'd never been into fitness and didn't have nearly as much strength as she needed. Every muscle from her neck to her hips strained with her effort, and it took every scrap of energy to pull herself up.

Inch by inch, she rose higher, her head poking up into the vent. Her hands gripped the rough edge so tightly that a line across her left palm began to bleed. With the fear of falling at the back of her mind, she gave a great heave, pulling her shoulders and hips into the vent. With a gust of air, she collapsed onto the solid surface, letting the cold seep into her skin and cool her.

She tried to survey the damage to her palm, but the wound was impossible to see. Another deep throaty scream came from the next room over, and Lynn was on the move. The pipe clanged against the metal, noting every few feet of progress she made.

The grate of a vent cover allowed her to peer down into the next room. It was the rec room again. She squinted, unable to make out more than a few shapes of long-forgotten furniture. Getting a grip on the pipe, Lynn adjusted the best she could in the small space and slid past the loose grate. It crashed to the ground. A gasp and a shuffle of footsteps, and Lynn was ready. With a sudden burst of bravery, Lynn leaped up, holding the pipe up.

The outline of a figure loomed nearby, and Lynn grasped the pipe even tighter in her sweaty hands. "Who are you?"

"Hey, whoa. Don't swing," a deep voice said, and the figure approached, hands held out cautiously.

"Stay back," she said and swung the pipe for good effect. A bloody corpse and now another person in the asylum? It couldn't be a coincidence. Lynn caught a glimpse of the side of his face in the weak moonlight and nearly dropped the pipe. "It's you," she said. When he screwed up his face, she added, "The weirdo from the ice cream shop. You're the one who kept staring at me."

The man blinked, eyes wide as if he were as shell-shocked as she was. He took a step backward, and she didn't know if that was due to the weapon she brandished or if he'd had a similar thought about her. Like alley cats, they did a semi-circle, eyeing and sizing up one another.

"Did you do this?" she demanded, gesturing to the body a few feet away with her elbow. From her peripheral, she tried to see through the door that led out of the room, the only means of escape if things turned ugly.

"No! No, no, no," he said, voice squeaky and high.

Lynn held tighter to her weapon. He was either telling the truth or a very good actor.

His eyes searched her face and her frame as if he were trying to pinpoint exactly where he'd seen her before. "She's…she's my friend."

"Your friend?"

"Yes. I was looking for her and my other friend, and I got lost in the woods." His eyes moved to her weapon again before returning to her. "How did... how did you get here?"

Lynn looked away sharply. The last thing she wanted to do was tell this stranger, a potentially dangerous man, that voices had lured her here. I got caught in the rain," she said quickly, hoping he wouldn't hear the waiver in her voice. She squeezed the pipe again. What were her odds of winning if he randomly charged at her?

Not good.

"I take it from that expression you found her a while ago," he continued, voice oddly deadpanned, and Lynn couldn't understand it. Losing a loved one was hard. Finding their mutilated remains even harder. So why did his voice sound so *flat*?

Shock can do that do a person, she reminded her. *But so can guilt.*

The hair on the back of her neck stood up, and she took the smallest half step backward, wondering if he would pursue her. "How'd you know to come here to search?

He looked away so sharply Lynn recoiled. What if he was searching for something to grab from the rubble? A weapon to combat her pipe.

"You're going to think I'm crazy."

Lynn tilted her head to the side, thinking of the perfect irony of being brought together by voices.

The corner of his lip twitched from her lack of a response. "Something about this place…something is *wrong* here. I…heard a voice. Calling to me in the woods." He ran a hand across his face. "That sounds so crazy."

"Not really. I hear them all the time," Lynn blurted out then stopped, wishing she could suck the words back into her throat and out of the air for him to hear. It felt like such a jump, a risk, to spill such an intimate secret to this stranger.

She expected him to look at her like she was crazy. Instead, his lips parted, and he stared at her as if she had suddenly become interesting. "You did?"

Now it was Lynn's turn to look away. She didn't want to see how his expression would change when she dropped the rest of the truth bomb. "I hear voices all the time," she said in a small voice. "A few years ago, I was diagnosed with schizophrenia. The meds have made it easier to manage, but sometimes, I still hear them."

The man's lips pressed together, and as she suspected, a tiny glint of disappointment shone in his eyes. "That's not crazy," he said. Then to clarify, he added, "*You're not crazy.*"

Lynn raised a questioning eyebrow, feeling as if he was simply being nice. Her mother and sister certainly thought she was crazy. Why would a perfect stranger not?

"The voice? I don't think it has anything to do with your condition. I think it's…tied to this place somehow," he said. "I found Kasey's car in the middle of the road when I nearly wrecked into it. He wasn't there so I thought he'd gotten hurt somehow and wandered into the woods. Then I heard this voice calling to me."

Lynn narrowed her eyes, suspicious. For all she knew, this could be one big prank—tourists trying to have fun with a local. They could've been the voices that had led her here. "It told you to come *here*?"

His face pulled tight as if remembering something particularly painful. "Something like that, yeah."

"I don't know what that voice is, but I know that once someone gets in here, there is no way out," Lynn said. "The front doors don't open, and I haven't found another exit yet."

"Sounds like you could use some help then." The man extended a large hand toward her. "I'm Jayden."

Wordlessly, Lynn stared at his hand. She couldn't push away the lingering thought it could all be a cruel prank. Or he was actually dangerous, and she'd caught a murderer in the middle of his dark deed.

If you walk away, he could plan something else. With him by your side, you can keep an eye on him.

It was the most practical thought she'd had yet.

Resigned, she returned the handshake. "I'm Lynn."

Chapter Twenty
Jayden

WHEN THE HANDSHAKE ended, Jayden continued to stare at this woman, thinking how odd it was that though he didn't know anything about her, he wanted to trust her. Lynn didn't seem to feel the same. She hadn't lowered her weapon during their entire encounter, but it didn't seem as if she'd hurt him. Though he couldn't say he'd blame her if she changed her mind. Clearly someone, or something here, *was* dangerous.

She could be, the tiny doubts in the back of his mind warned. *These secluded towns are great for breeding weirdos. She's already said she's mentally ill.*

"Do you...do you need a minute alone before we go?" she asked, pulling him from his thoughts.

Jayden didn't know how to answer at first. He took a breath, trying to calm his frantic heartbeat and process all the information the last ten minutes had thrown his way. If that really was Kay's body, then Kasey had to be around here too.

Maybe it's not her, he told himself. Jayden inched toward the shadows in the corner of the room, the moonlight from the ceiling revealing a glint of a ring on her finger. The same one she had a habit of fidgeting with, and he couldn't bury his doubts anymore.

"Please," he said at last.

Lynn bowed her head and slipped across the room, disappearing into the shadows before her footsteps creaked in the hall. Jayden watched her, wondering where she'd go. Maybe she wouldn't even wait for him at all and would resume her search for an exit.

I'll be a minute behind, he thought. *But this comes first.*

Jayden liked to pride himself on his ability to handle devastating news with ease. Ever since his brother had been killed in the war, not much hurt him. He navigated the world at a distance, keeping everything at arm's length to avoid all possible pain.

Now, while looking down at the remains of his friend, he realized he hadn't been as successful with it as he'd thought. Jayden crouched down, putting two fingers to the curve of her neck, ever hopeful that his previous search had been too hasty to prove real results. Like last time, no pulse thrummed. Her skin was ragged, torn and bloody. It felt warm, but not the normal kind of warm. Whatever life had been left was leaking out. The same overwhelming pain from his brother's death crashed over him at the realization, and he couldn't stop it. Couldn't push the pain away.

It was like someone shoved a white-hot nail into his heart. He couldn't breathe. An ugly weeping sound made its way into his throat, and thick tears scorched his face. Someone had done something to her. If it hadn't been the mysterious girl he'd let leave the room, then she was in danger too, and he'd let her go right back into the thick of it. Carefully, he shifted, sure to touch the floor as little as possible. Jayden had never been the religious type. He had no idea how to start out a prayer, but this was his friend.

"Whatever happened to you, I'm so sorry," he said in hushed whispers. "I promise to personally track down whoever did this and make them pay."

Lynn emerged from the shadows, lip tucked in her teeth. "I don't know if I should tell you this."

Jayden blinked, confused by the intrusion. He'd been so sure she'd left, he hadn't listening for her coming back. What could possibly be said that they hadn't already discussed? He briefly considered the idea that *she* had done this to his friends, but he didn't want to believe it.

It makes sense, he thought begrudgingly.

"Tell me what?" he asked at last, bracing himself.

"What did this to your friend...I don't think it was human," she said, staring down at the floor as if she didn't want to say the words out loud.

Jayden drew his eyebrows together, more convinced his original theory had legs after all. "What else could it be?"

Lynn shrugged, looking somehow smaller. "I don't know, but when I heard...the screams, I tried to come and save her, but something kept me away. I didn't...I didn't see what it was."

Jayden frowned, not knowing if he believed her or not. "How'd you get away?"

Lynn looked over her shoulder, toward the open door

as if she expected something to appear at any minute. Jayden's spine went rigid with unease as Lynn said, "It... disappeared."

Jayden physically bit his tongue to keep himself from speaking. Any words he could say wouldn't be kind. It was one thing to think an animal had done this, a stray dog or maybe even a bear.

"You're saying *what* exactly?" he asked, trying to stay patient while at the same time not pulling it off very well. "That a-a ghost did this?"

"We can have this conversation later. We need to get away from this room *now*."

Jayden wanted to unleash every ounce of anger he'd kept under wraps since the trip began. In the low light, he caught the expression on her face, the fear, and thought maybe she was right.

Something supernatural is at work here, he reminded himself.

Unwilling to further the argument, Jayden said, "Fine. Let's go," and pushed past her. She stayed rooted to the spot, and he turned to face her. "What?"

"I can tell there's something you're not saying. I mean, you don't believe me, about the monster, but you won't say as much. Why? What happened to you in the woods?"

Jayden rolled his eyes upward until he stared at the ceiling. He couldn't tell this girl what had happened. He couldn't tell *anyone*. His sanity depended on it. "You'll think

I'm crazy."

Lynn laughed, matching him step for step when he tried to turn away. "We've had this conversation already. I'm the *Queen* of Crazy, remember?"

Jayden shook his head and turned to make his way down the hall. They didn't have time to argue. They needed to figure something out and *fast*.

Lynn followed him, her irritated voice filling the corridor along with their footsteps. "Hey!" she called. "Tell me what happened!"

Jayden walked faster, drawn to the lobby and the tiny bit of moonlight seeping in from outside. With any luck, the entrance would be open this time. Jayden slammed into the doors with his shoulder. When that didn't work, he pounded his fists on it until they radiated pain. Gritting his teeth, Jayden pounded harder and harder, trying to dislodge all he'd seen. Tears threatened to bubble in his eyes, but he didn't let them fall. By the time Lynn caught up, his fists felt thoroughly bruised. He slid down the wall, feet spread out before him.

Lynn approached him like a wildcat, eyes alight with fire. "Hey! I'm talking to you!"

Jayden squeezed his eyes shut. "I know. I heard you."

"Then the polite thing to do is respond. Or at least acknowledge the person speaking."

Jayden tilted his head back, resting the top of his head to the door as he stared up at the ceiling. "Okay, but when I tell you, and you don't believe me, that's on you."

Lynn stared him down, expression not changing.

Jayden closed his eyes. "I wasn't completely honest...when I told you my story earlier," he began. "It was more than... a voice I heard. I had an entire vision. I heard someone call to me. I thought it was Kasey, so I followed it. Next thing I knew, it was daytime, and there were other people with me, but they weren't people I'd ever met before. It was like I was seeing the world through someone else's eyes or in a memory from someone else's head."

Lynn's back straightened and some of the irritation bled away. "Did it...feel like you were a prisoner in someone else's body?"

Jayden narrowed his eyes, unable to decide if she was toying him or being serious. "Yeah. Yeah, it did."

"I had my own...experience shortly before I found you."

Jayden's shoulders slumped with relief. If he was going to be branded insane, at least he wouldn't wear it alone.

"Did you know who any of the people in your vision were?"

"Wish I knew. There were two guys with him. I'd guess they were brothers, but I can't really say for sure. They were hunting something. Said something about a deer stand."

Lynn went rigid, morphing into a statue right before Jayden's eyes. "Was one of them blond with a ponytail? A little mole on his cheek?"

Jayden tilted his head to the side, bringing the man to mind and wondering how it could be possible she knew him. *Is she psychic?* he wondered. If things had already gotten this crazy, what was a little more? "Yeah. And another had had—"

"Brown hair."

"Yes," Jayden said again. "How...how are you doing this? You're freaking me out."

Lynn didn't look mystified by the realization or even angry like she'd been. It had all gone away leaving a sad glint in her eyes that Jayden didn't quite understand.

She's a local, he reminded himself. And then things made sense. "Wait. Did you *know* them?"

Lynn pursed her lips but didn't answer. When Jayden remembered the end of the flashback, he understood. In as soft a tone he could manage, he asked, "Who was he?"

"His name was Damien," Lynn said and plopped down on the floor beside him. "He was my boyfriend."

"Oh," Jayden said and blinked, the words really sinking in. "Oh, God, I'm sorry."

"They said his death was an accident," she said, meeting his gaze. "But I...never believed that."

Jayden kept quiet, waiting for her to continue.

"Did your flashback tell you...I mean, do you know how he died?"

Jayden remembered the roar of the unseen monster and the blast of a shotgun a second before the vision cut to black. "His cousin...the one with the ponytail shot him,"

Jayden said and found he couldn't look directly in her eyes. "We were running from something." He didn't want to mention he'd turned into the thing they were running from.

Lynn drew her face tight. "What was it?"

"I don't know. I never got a good look at it. I heard it though. It sounded like a bear."

Lynn's lip trembled, and she somehow went pale enough for her skin to glow unhealthily in the low light. "Did it sound like the thing in here? The thing that took your friend?"

It did. It *really* did, but Jayden didn't want to say as much. "This is crazy," he said instead.

Lynn scoffed. "Of course it is, but that doesn't mean it's not real. We were lured here for some reason. Something is trying to tell us a story, and we'd be damn fools not to listen."

Chapter Twenty-One
Lynn

LYNN SAT DOWN beside Jayden, staring at his profile. In the low light, his features were more prominent, the curve of his lips standing out more than it had when she'd seen him in daylight. There was no doubt that he was an attractive guy, his appearance amplified by his resemblance to Damien. The thought that Damien's spirit might've presented itself to him, hit her hard.

If Jayden was being honest, and Damien had somehow possessed him, why had he not presented himself to her?

Did I do something wrong?

Her skin crawled with the memory of the woman who had shown herself to Lynn. Who was she? And why had she chosen *Lynn* to pass her memories to?

"I've heard that when someone dies a particularly terrible death, their spirit gets trapped on Earth," Lynn said. "Maybe that's the connection. That's why we can't leave. They don't want us to."

"Makes about as much sense as the rest of this," Jayden said, running his finger over the dusty floor.

"The voice I heard was a woman. I think she used to be a patient here. She was running from a man. I've never felt so much fear before."

Jayden adjusted his position so that he could better look at her. "Did he kill her?"

"Can't say for sure. The memory just...*ended*," Lynn said, remembering how certain she'd been that the man would find her.

Grunting, Jayden stood up, offering her a hand. Lynn looked up at him, wishing she had an idea what he was thinking. "The only way to find out is to investigate."

Lynn took his hand, and Jayden helped her up before he moved on his way down the hall. Lynn hesitated before following. Even the hunch of his shoulders looked so similar to Damien that she wanted to cry.

She must've made a noise in her throat because Jayden turned to look at her over his shoulder. "Are you okay?"

Lynn hurried to wipe her face though he wouldn't be able to see much anyway. "Yeah, I...if Damien could contact *you*, I can't help but wonder why he hasn't...well, why he hasn't tried to reach out to me."

Jayden gaped, visibly struggling for words before he said, "Maybe he's tried?"

Lynn fell silent, thinking of all that had happened over the past twelve hours. Could it be that Damien had been the reason the terrible creature had stayed away from her?

The thought caused the slightest blossom of hope surging in her chest, and she wanted to hold onto it forever. "Yeah, maybe," she said as they walked back down the hall. Empty gurneys lined the walls and a discarded blanket had been cast over the path. Mold and decay made the air heavy and hard to breathe in.

"Half of this place doesn't look like anything's wrong with it," Jayden said, kicking the blanket to the side.

Lynn gave him a sideways look. "Well, it's not as if the entire place went up in flames. It was only one wing."

Jayden raised an eyebrow, not looking convinced.

"What?"

"That doesn't seem odd to you?"

Lynn frowned. She'd thought finding the building at all to be strange. "You think someone lit the fire intentionally?"

"Maybe," Jayden pondered. "What do you know about this place? I mean, you grew up around here, right?"

"West Gate used to be a place where people stored their unwanted people."

"Do you think anyone was killed here?"

"Who knows? The rumor mill has made so many stories about this place, it's hard to tell fact from fiction. Until today, I used to think the entire place burned to the ground. No one's talked much about it in years."

"So why not tear it down?"

"The deed was lost so legally...they can't. They planted trees to try and hide it, and for the most part, the town forgot it was a real place."

Lynn paused to glance inside the nearest room. It was neat, standardized, with a tiny dresser and hospital bed. There was a tiny window with bars over it and a small closet barely large enough to hang a few outfits inside.

"It looks like jail," Lynn said, shaking her head.

Jayden said nothing, pressing his lips into a grim line that made her wonder what he was thinking. As they continued down the hall, the smell of ash grew stronger.

"Do you think we'll be able to get out through the burned wing?" he asked.

"It's a possibility."

Before Lynn could say another word, her head swirled with drowsiness, violent vertigo sweeping through her and changing the dim ashy hallway to its restored state. Loud shrieking filled the space around her, and it took a minute to realize *she* was the one making the sound.

Except it wasn't her. It was the woman again. The lights highlighted the clinical white walls as she was dragged down the hall. The grip on her upper arms tightened as she struggled, and she tried to glance over her shoulder. The man she'd run from in her last flashback held her tight, face twisted into a malicious sneer.

"You've been a bad girl," he said. "And you know what happens to bad girls."

Lynn didn't, and she didn't *want* to know. This woman though, whoever she was, knew perfectly well. She wailed even louder, gaining a few stares from patients they passed. No one spoke in her defense, most of them dropping eye contact as soon as the doctor's gaze scorched over them.

The room he took her to was clean though it smelled musty and full of old disinfectants as if someone had broken a bottle rather than used it to clean. There were two bathtubs, one on either side of the room. A heavy cloth sat over top of each one, secured to the floor with black straps.

Lynn held her breath, able to guess what would come next. Old asylums would punish patients by submerging them in a bathtub filled with either ice or boiling water. The patient would be stuck until their punisher set them free. Based on the fear in her spirit guest, this wasn't her first experience here.

The man held her with an arm across her abdomen, using his other hand to pull back the cover. Sharp, uneven chunks of ice sat inside. She struggled, desperately trying to break free, and he laughed which only made her struggle harder. Before she could escape, she was inside the contraption, the ice sinking into her backside and freezing her.

The man sneered at her and dropped the cloth, securing it in place. The woman struggled to keep her chin up, her hands desperately pushing the fabric from the inside. The man watched, intrigued, until screaming sounded from the hallway.

"Raid!" someone, another doctor judging from the look of his outfit, screamed as he sprinted past the room.

The doctor who had trapped the woman in the ice bath gave her a final twisted smile before he ran, not looking back. Her heart pounded so hard it hurt. So hard, Lynn wondered if a heart attack had been what had done this girl in.

"Help!" she screamed, pushing harder on the thick cloth.

It didn't budge.

"Help!" she yowled again, desperate to be heard though she had the feeling she was too far away from anyone who could help.

No one came, and a horrible sensation washed over her—the smell of smoke. A second later came the crackle of flames. The fire hadn't reached her room yet, but it would soon. More people sprinted down the hallway, not a single one noticing her.

"Help!" Lynn tried again, the smell of burning material choking her.

When smoke filtered into the room, real panic set in. She coughed, struggles beginning to weaken as the air thinned. When the first orange-red flames licked up the wall, spreading toward the ceiling, cold defeat bubbled in her stomach. Lynn sobbed a second before a beam in the ceiling came loose, crashing to the ground and cutting her world to black.

Chapter Twenty-Two
Jayden

JAYDEN'S EYES WENT wide as he waved a hand in front of Lynn's face. She didn't move, hadn't in a good minute or two. Her eyes were huge, glazed over as if she were staring into a memory, and he wondered if she was having some sort of episode.

What do I do?

"Lynn!" he screamed, hoping to pull her back from whatever place she'd slipped away to.

He wanted to grab her and shake her, to snap her out of the trance by force, but he didn't know if that was a good idea or not. If this was anything like sleepwalking, he'd be better leaving her alone.

This is worse than sleepwalking, he thought, reaching for her.

He pulled his hand back at the last second. He didn't know what to do for her. He wanted this to stop. Jayden looked over his shoulder, wondering if he could find anything nearby. When his gaze landed back on her, she gasped as if she hadn't breathed in the last five minutes, eyes coming back to focus.

"Hey, hey," he soothed, trying to ease her out of her shock. "It's me. You're safe."

Her pupils, blown from whatever she'd experienced,

started to shrink back to normal size. "I saw her...how she died."

He didn't have to ask *who,* it was apparent by the haunted look in her eyes.

"There was a raid on the hospital. I think...I think one of the doctors set the fire to try and destroy any evidence of misconduct. The woman...she was trapped there when the wing went up."

"That's horrible."

Lynn turned away, and Jayden didn't ask any more questions. If she needed a minute to process what she'd seen, that was something he could give. She started to walk, staying ahead of him a few steps at all times as if she didn't want him to see her face. As they crossed into the burned wing, Jayden stared at her back, wanting to tell her to be cautious.

He bit it back. She was on a mission, and he didn't want to do a thing to interrupt it.

Lynn wove through piles of rubble and down the twisting remains of burned halls. He was baffled, lost by the blackened structures. Some had crumbled to rubble and ash while others remained intact. Both facts didn't slow her down.

They stopped only when they reached the room with the two porcelain claw-foot bathtubs. A surge of despair coursed through Jayden. If the woman had really died here shortly before it was abandoned, it was possible that she was *still* here.

Lynn must've had the same thought because she kept the fire in her steps as she headed to the bathtub on the left side of the room. Wood sat across the top of it, rubble and tiny pieces of wood littering the floor around it. She grabbed the beam, wrapping her hands around it before she pulled, straining so hard the veins bulged in her neck. When that didn't work, she rammed her shoulder into it.

"Lynn, don't do it," Jayden said. "You aren't going to want to see what's in there."

"Help me," she growled through clenched teeth.

Knowing he wouldn't win the argument, Jayden took his place on the opposite side of the tub. He grabbed the beam, doing his best to not get any splinters in the process. Together, they inched it centimeter by centimeter until gravity claimed it. It crashed to the floor, causing Jayden to stumble away with the fear it would crush his foot.

Lynn's hands worked the binds holding the cover in place. Before Jayden could stop her, she pulled it aside and gasped, raising a hand to cover her mouth. Jayden forced himself to glance inside. A decaying pile of bones sat at the bottom of the basin, the smell of sickly-sweet death rising from it.

"She died here, all alone," Lynn said, letting go of the cover to hug herself as if she were suddenly cold.

Jayden stared at the floor, unsure how he felt. While Damien's death had been brutal, he'd at least spent his last few minutes in the company of loved ones. This woman had spent that time in fear.

Life really isn't fair.

Jayden wanted to say something comforting, something that could soothe both of them, but he didn't know if that was possible. Seeing the bones was jarring, of course, but the idea that ghosts were real and that they had chosen to speak to them hit him harder.

"There's nothing we can do for her now," he said at last, trying to catch Lynn's eye.

She wouldn't look at him. She shook her head from side to side, swinging her curly hair around her shoulders. "I don't think that's true. If her spirit is still here then it's because of this. Maybe she showed herself to me because somehow I *can* help her."

"How?" Jayden asked, barely holding in his skepticism. If anything, she should be trying to help him get them out of the asylum.

"I don't know. Give her a proper burial?"

"Do you really think she lured you all the way out here for that?"

"If I was murdered, I'd want someone to find me. To find the truth," Lynn said, voice hoarse as if she were holding in a sob.

Jayden pursed his lips, suddenly guilty. By the look in her eye, he could tell she was thinking of Damien. The guilt she felt over his death was transferring to this mystery woman.

"You can't blame yourself, you know."

"Huh?"

"I know what you're doing," Jayden said, bringing himself to gently grab her shoulders. "You're paying homage to Damien by focusing on this woman, but she's not him. This isn't going to bring him back."

Lynn's hands tightened into fists at her sides, and she shrugged him off. "Don't you think I know that? This is the right thing to do."

Jayden winced.

"Besides, it might all be connected," Lynn said. "Her and the doctor and the monster? We're missing something. And if we figure it out, the spirits might let us out of here."

"How in the world do you propose they're connected?" Jayden asked with a scoff. "You think this doctor made a monster out of people like his own version of *Human Centipede*?"

"I don't know, and that's the part that scares me," she admitted.

"If you think appeasing the ghosts will give us a shot of getting out of here, it's worth a try, I suppose," Jayden said flatly, "but first and foremost, let's keep it in our heads to find an emergency exit."

Lynn stood rigid for a second, staring at the bathtub as if she wanted to argue. Instead, her eyes went glassy and she whispered, "I'm sorry for what's happened to you," before she let Jayden guide her out of the room.

Chapter Twenty-Three
Lynn

LYNN AND JAYDEN left the room, not feeling much better about the trip ahead of them. He occasionally ducked into rooms, still on the lookout for his missing friend while Lynn's mind was a million miles away.

How do you put someone to rest who's been dead for over a hundred years? Lynn wondered.

Suddenly, she'd found herself glad for all the occult books she'd checked out from the library as a teenager. The information would come in handy now. According to most of those books, the way to destroy a spirit would be to put the body to rest or carry out their unfinished business.

So what now?

"Any idea where the doctor could've gone?"

Lynn frowned, squeezing her eyes shut to try and bring the scene from the woman's final moments to the front of her brain. The last glimpse she'd had of him was him ducking into the hallway. In her mind's eye, she would swear he had taken a left which would put him deeper in the wing.

Lynn opened her mouth when the earsplitting roar of the invisible beast shook the room.

Jayden's eyes went so wide they looked like two black pits. "We have to hide."

Lynn did a three-sixty. The only spot that would

come close to a hiding place would be backtracking to the room with the bathtubs. The thought of curling up next to the woman's remains made Lynn want to retch. Jayden must've had the same thought because he darted out into the hall. Lynn tried to keep up, but the piles of rubble and debris made it difficult. They ducked through the moonlight and back into the shadows. Lynn tried not to focus on the sounds behind her, following Jayden by his ragged gasps for air as they blazed through the hall.

An entire roar came from behind her, and Lynn cried out, afraid to look back. Afraid that if she did, she *would* see the beast, and it would be close enough to claim her. Flashes of the remains of Jayden's friend filled her mind, sending a chill down her spine. Despite the blood, she couldn't help but wonder if she'd died of fear first or if the thing had physically stolen the life from her.

Either way, she didn't want to share her fate.

A pile of charred rubble blocked the hallway ahead, and she panicked, eyeing the gaps. None of them looked particularly large enough to get through, but Jayden had disappeared this way two seconds ahead of her.

He made it. I can too.

Escape wouldn't be easy, but panic made her willing to try anything. She charged toward the biggest gap, forcing her body through. The stones dug into her skin and clothes. Her shirt ripped at the sleeve, sagging on her shoulder. Coughing from the dust, she thought the stones would keep her in place forever.

Lynn lunged forward, the momentum enough to get through. She landed on her side, jolts of pain coming from her hip and shoulder, but she was otherwise okay. Plaster fell in chunks around her, the only sound as the roaring subsided.

She sat up, tossing her hair over her shoulder as she peeked at the rubble, convinced she'd see a monster staring back at her. A handful of dust caused her to cough again.

"Jayden!" she called, looking around frantically when she didn't spot him.

This room was cold and dark, void of all windows.

It's the solitary room, one of her voices told her.

She shivered. Lynn had always imagined a padded cell would be, well, padded. This wasn't. The entire hospital hadn't looked remotely close to comfortable, but this room was somehow ten times worse. Lynn breathed out, and the air around her dropped in temperature.

Teeth chattering, she wrapped her arms across her chest and paced to the end of the room to see if she was wrong about her surroundings. She'd been so sure Jayden had gone this way, but she'd lost him.

Lynn turned and froze, sucking in a gasp of air. Light filtered in from the tiny remains of a window that hadn't fully collapsed on the other side of the rubble. The figure standing in the beam of moonlight had its back to her, but she'd recognize the hair, the curve of the neck, the body posture anywhere.

"Damien?" she whispered.

He turned toward her. Damien's face was so real, so ethereal, that Lynn wanted to cry out with pleasure. The image of Damien beckoned to her, a smile on his face. His arms lifted, and in the back of her mind, she could hear his voice calling to her though his lips didn't move as he said it.

Through her ecstasy, the hair on the back of Lynn's neck rose. Her initial reaction was to run to him, to fall into his outstretched arms. How she missed snuggling with him, being as close to another human being as physically possible.

But this wasn't right.

Whatever she was seeing, this couldn't be him. He was *dead.* Had been for a long time.

Time doesn't move back, only forward.

Once the light of a person's soul burned out from the center of their vessel, there was no way to reignite it.

"You're not him," she whispered and took a shaky step backward. One tiny tear coursed down her cheek when the face morphed.

"Of course I am, baby," he said softly, his smile warm and inviting though something in his eyes shifted.

Lynn took another step backward, hands pressed to the wall. She shook her head from side to side, once then twice.

The smile on Damien's face grew even wider as his beautiful brown eyes shifted into black pits. It stared into Lynn's eyes for a solid thirty seconds before dissipating into a flurry of a hundred white souls, beings lost by the sands of time.

Lynn cried out, unsure if she was afraid or heartbroken. The rollercoaster of seeing Damien and having him ripped away five minutes later tore open all her old wounds. She tried to stifle her sobs by holding a sleeve over her hand, but it echoed around the empty room, somehow louder when it came back to her.

"Lynn!"

Lynn perked up, dashing across the room. Never before would she think she'd be so happy to hear a stranger over Damien's voice.

"I'm here!" she cried, grabbing the rubble to throw a few chunks to the side. In the low light, it was hard to find the hole she'd slid through.

"Lynn!" Jayden cried again.

Lynn stepped up onto the concrete, peering through the gap. Jayden's eyes glinted as he peered back.

"Are you okay?" he asked, reaching a hand through.

Lynn grabbed it, allowing him to pull her through to the other side. He let go, and she patted herself down, accidentally touching the cut on her arm.

"Yeah, yeah. I'm fine."

"I thought something happened. One minute you were at my side, and the next, you were gone."

"Short legs," Lynn said, trying to laugh, but she couldn't bring herself to do it.

"Did something...happen?"

"No."

Studying the hallway around them, she noticed the break that led down the turn in the hall that she'd missed earlier.

Jayden followed her gaze. "I've got some good news at least," he said, clapping his hand on her shoulder. "I think I might've found something to help us."

Chapter Twenty-Four
Jayden

AS JAYDEN AND Lynn walked side by side down the hall, he couldn't help but glance at her. There was a glaze in her eyes, something that suggested she was on the verge of a breakdown. Something had happened to her in the brief time they'd been separated, but she wouldn't tell him what.

Did she see Kasey? he wondered. If she'd found his other friend, surely, she would let him know?

He glanced at her, just as uncertain. He thought about asking again, trying a different approach to see if she was close enough to the breaking point to spill it all.

"We're a pair," he said out loud before he could stop himself.

Lynn turned to him, eyes narrowed and face sharp as if she'd been offended by the statement. "What do you mean by that?"

"That you can tell me if something happened," he said. "I know I don't...I don't *know* you, but you seem reserved. Like you're used to being by yourself or keeping things to yourself. We're a lot alike in that aspect."

"That's got to be the best spin on a shit situation I've ever heard. I envy you that."

The comment made him sad, and he wasn't entirely

sure why. He wanted to tell her that there was no reason to envy him, that his life had been a shitshow for years, but she probably wouldn't believe him.

"Are you gonna tell me what you found?" she asked when he said nothing.

"Back in the day, they didn't have a fancy computer to help them keep track of all their patient files, right?" Jayden began. "They had to do that manually. So, they needed somewhere to keep their paperwork. Say, an entire room."

"You found it?"

Jayden nodded as they walked through a doorframe. The door was long gone, and Jayden didn't stop to wonder where it could've gone. He held his hand out, blocking her from moving forward another step. She glanced at him, and he gestured with his chin to the drop in the middle of the room. The floor at the edge of the room still held in place, creating an eerie frame around the blackness in the middle of the floor. The tiles curved downward, and Lynn wondered how deep of a drop it was.

Lynn looked suspicious when she glanced back up at him. "How do you know anything's down there at all?"

He shrugged, staring down into the blackness. "I don't. Not really, but it's my best guess. I mean, why go through the trouble of trying to burn *this* part of the hospital rather than any other wing? If they were looking to destroy the entire building, they could've set fire to the second floor, but they didn't. They chose *this* wing."

Lynn reached into her pocket, fiddling for something. A tiny click and then an orange flame emerged, highlighting the curve of her face. She tried to hold the lighter toward the hole, enough to see anything through the blackness, but the tiny flame wasn't enough.

"Get a glimpse of anything?" Lynn asked as soon as the tiny orange spark went out.

Jayden shook his head. "Where'd you get that?"

"You dropped it earlier."

"Oh," Jayden said, patting his pockets down. He hadn't noticed it was even missing.

She dropped to her hands and knees, pressing herself as close to the edge as she could without falling in. "See anything now?" she asked, straining her arm at an angle that looked almost painful.

"No, noth—"

Lynn's hold loosened, and she slid toward the opening, screaming out as blackness reclaimed the room. Jayden fell to his hands and knees, desperate to grab any part of her. He missed. His eyes went wide at the sound of impact, and he bayed at the edge of the hole, contemplating between jumping in after her and searching for a nearby exit to get help.

"Lynn! Lynn! Can you hear me?"

A low groan echoed up from the darkness, and Jayden let out a little puff of air. At least she hadn't died on impact.

"Are you okay?" he called.

A groan and a shuffle. Lynn hissed through her teeth, and rubble clattered, before she replied, "As good as I'm going to be."

"Nothing broken? No blood?"

"I'll be fine," she assured him, and to prove her point, she lit the lighter again, holding it up for him to get a glimpse of her face.

She stood beside a downed ceiling beam, the ground around her littered with the remains of paper and glass. "Looks like you were right."

"What else do you see?"

Lynn scanned her surroundings, her position documented by the tiny orange flame moving in rhythm with herself. "A lot of the stuff is burned. You were right about the origin of the fire." She took a step forward, footsteps crunching against hard pieces of plaster. "There are plenty of file cabinets down here though."

"Any of them that survived?"

A minute of silence as Lynn moved through the burned room. He heard the rattle of her grasping the knob, and a second later, it opened with a *woosh*.

"I think they all did. They might've been fireproof."

"And the doctor didn't know that?"

"It's probably not information the hospital would share," Lynn said over the ruffle of pages as she started to look through the drawer.

"Perfect," he said, squinting. "Is there a good place for me to jump? I'm coming down."

"Don't go directly in the center. There's a sharp piece of wood sticking up at the perfect angle to spear somebody who's not careful."

Jayden cringed. Grasping onto the floor, he let his feet dangle into the hole and inched backward. When gravity started to pull him down, his grip grew stronger before he convinced himself to let go and landed on his back with a thump. Tiny pieces of gravel and debris dug into his skin, but he felt no pain.

"You okay?" Lynn asked.

"Yeah," Jayden said, patting away the dust as he stood. Following the light from the lighter, he crossed the room, and touched the cold metal on the side of the cabinet she rummaged through. "We got lucky with these."

Lynn shrugged as she plucked a file from the drawer. "It was the 19th century. They probably didn't know what *fireproof* was."

"Fair enough," Jayden said, tipping his head to read the name on the file. "What's it say?"

"Teresa Gray," Lynn started to read. "Age forty-three. Brought in for a sudden bout of silence and melancholy after the death of her newborn child."

Jayden wrinkled his nose. "They hospitalized people for that?"

Lynn scoffed and peered up at him over the edge of the folder. "Back then, they hospitalized women for everything."

"That's not right," Jayden said glancing to the drawer

and the faint outline of the other cabinets nearby. How many files inside of them contained information about women trying to cope with a tragedy in their lives?

"It gets worse," Lynn said. "Says she didn't respond to the treatment, so their *methods* went a little more unorthodox. When those didn't work, they decided she was simply beyond help and..." She paused, bringing the file closer to her face as if she couldn't believe the words that had been written.

"What did they do?" Jayden asked, unsure if he really wanted to know.

"They *experimented* on her."

"Jesus," Jayden said, shaking his head. "At least that confirms the rumors that people died here."

Lynn flipped through a few pages. "It doesn't say *when* she died though."

"They might not have been smart about a lot of things. But when it came to covering their tracks, they were right on top of it. They would know better than to make it look as if they were responsible for her death. They probably forged this paperwork to make it look as if everything was fine should anyone happen to look into it."

Lynn closed the folder, setting it on top of the cabinet and started to read the next one.

Jayden peeked into the drawer. There were at least twenty more files inside of it. He tried to imagine the hundreds, possibly thousands, of files the room might hold, and felt small. "How are we gonna find your girl in all these cabinets?" he finally brought himself to ask. "Do you know her name?"

Lynn looked thoughtful. "No, I don't. I know her thoughts and her feelings and her memories, but I don't even know what she looks like."

Jayden tilted his head to the side. "Well, I guess it's a good thing we're trapped in this building since we'll be here for a while anyway." He plucked the first file from the drawer and plopped down among the rubble, beginning to read.

Chapter Twenty-Five
Lynn

LYNN WATCHED JAYDEN for a minute before she grabbed a folder and sat beside him. It didn't take long for them to fall into companionable silence as they read, the stack of manila folders and papers between them growing larger with each passing minute. Each story Lynn read made her feel worse—women who were hospitalized for depression, women hospitalized because they liked sex, women hospitalized because they wouldn't *bow* to their husbands.

All of it left a bad feeling in the pit of her stomach about what it really meant to get *treatment* of any kind. She'd always known asylums were horror shows. Even in the twenty-first century, things still weren't on the up and up. Lynn put herself in the shoes of every woman whose story she read. Her heart filled with their pain, her head filled with their terror, and as she shut the last file in the drawer, she didn't think she could take anymore.

"I can't read any more of these. They're horrific," Jayden said.

Lynn picked up another folder. "Yeah, they're pretty rough."

"There's a woman who was injected with chemicals to try to make her *calm* because she didn't love her husband anymore. It's no wonder this place is haunted. It reeks of evil."

"You've got that right."

The file seemed so light, so small, and yet Lynn knew that the information contained in it wasn't. It was heavy, haunted with all that remained of a woman who had lived a tragic life and died an even more tragic death.

Lynn puffed her cheeks, the hand with the lighter shaking as she read the name on the cover. Victoria White. The name sounded so normal, so regal. The first page in the file was yellow, the writing so smudged and faded it was almost illegible. Lynn squinted, trying her best to make out what it said.

The first line was the woman's name followed by her age, weight, height, and physical description. Lynn took a minute to study the details of her appearance—brown hair, blue eyes, widow's peak in her hair—and tried to picture her. It was still so odd to know a person so thoroughly without knowing what they looked like.

Her eyes drifted to the next line, the reason why Victoria had been committed: *hears voices*. Lynn stared at the words, not processing them at first. When the reality started to sink in, she closed the folder, letting the lighter go out as she stared at the wall through the shadows.

"What is it?" Jayden asked. "What does it say?"

Lynn had never really thought much about the afterlife before. Of course her mother and Amelia were Christian, believing in everything that comes after life, and

Lynn wanted to believe it if for no one but Damien. No matter how much she tried though, Lynn had never been as sold as them. She had read a philosophy book before that referenced people like her as an "embodiment of multiple souls." That stuck with her. If God was real, why would he want to punish people by sticking several of them inside the same person?

It seemed cruel. Unnecessarily so.

"Her name was Victoria," Lynn whispered at last. "The reason she was here, the reason she was tortured and murdered, was because she heard voices. She was schizophrenic. Just like me."

"Oh," Jayden said, the wind knocked from his sails as an awkward silence hung over them.

Lynn couldn't blame him for it. She hardly knew what to say herself.

"Now that we know the truth, what do we do next?" Jayden asked. "If it was up to me, I'd say we torch the entire place."

"That's the easy answer," Lynn said thoughtfully. "Maybe if we get rid of this place, and everything in it, everyone who's trapped here will be set free."

Jayden agreed and glanced up at the room above them. "Only problem now is getting back out of here."

The edges of the hole were barely visible but gauging the distance from when she'd fallen in, they wouldn't be able to jump back out.

"We'll have to make something to climb," Lynn

decided at last. "There's plenty of stuff down here, and if it comes down to it, we can use the cabinets."

"I'm game."

Together, they gathered the biggest pieces of wood they could find. The resulting pile was lumpy and didn't reach as high as they needed to go, but Lynn supposed it would work in a pinch. She poked it, watching the entire thing threaten to crumble. Falling from this into the rubble could be treacherous if they landed on any sharp pieces they failed to notice.

"You first," Jayden said, and Lynn wondered if he'd had the same thought. "I'll help push you up when you get to the top."

Lynn took one step forward and paused, doubt seeping through her again. They'd survived everything so far so this should be easy.

You've done worse.

She draped her sleeves over her hands, cautious of splinters or nails, and started to climb. Shuffling behind her told her Jayden was close, ready to catch her if she slipped. Lynn hurried to the top, queasy with the way it rocked under their combined weight. She looked at the floor looming above them. Breathing through her nose to keep from going into a full anxiety attack, she willed her hands to let go and shifted her weight to her haunches. The board beneath her shifted, and she whimpered.

Jayden rested a hand on the middle of her back, holding her in place. "I won't let you fall."

"I don't know if this is going to work," Lynn admitted, peering at him over her shoulder.

"Want me to go first?"

"No, I can do this."

"Okay. Don't think you *have* to. I'll switch whenever you want."

Lynn focused on how comforting his voice was as she rose, standing to her full height. She was ready to cheer when the board beneath her moved again, this time slipping so quickly, it took her down with it. Stomach lurching, she screamed out, listening to the thump as Jayden tried to grab her and fell too. Lynn crashed to the floor, her head smacking against the wall as she came to a rest.

"Lynn!" Jayden cried, a few feet away.

To her, he sounded miles away down a long tunnel. She didn't respond. *Couldn't* respond. She watched as a rusty door a few feet away fell from its eroded hinges—a decaying skeleton following close behind.

Chapter Twenty-Six
Jayden

EVERYTHING IN JAYDEN froze. Lynn's body hit the floor with a thump so loud it made him sick. If something happened to her, something that incapacitated her, he didn't know how they'd get out of this room let alone the entire hospital.

Why did I push her to go first?

A door blocked him from her, and he moved it to the side, realizing it wasn't the only thing that lay between them. There was a body or the remains of one. He screamed and tossed it out of his path as fast as he could. Wiping his hands on his clothes, he tried to rid his skin of the grimy sensation as he dropped to his knees beside Lynn.

The door hadn't been too heavy, but he worried that between it and the fall, she'd been knocked unconscious. A streak of blood matted the hair to her temple. Muttering curses under his breath, Jayden looked around but saw nothing that could potentially help either of them out of this jam. Setting a hand to the side of her face, he tried to see her eyes, uncertain of what to do.

If she died here, it'd be his fault.

It was your idiot plan to build the unsafe thing.

"Lynn, please," he said, pulling his hand back.

Her head slumped forward, chin resting against her

chest.

This way, a tiny voice called to him.

Jayden's spine went rigid, and when he turned to look at who was there, a flash of light blinded him. He blinked to clear it, and when his vision returned, the room was lit, fully restored to its original condition a century before. The cabinets were shiny and new, and Jayden shivered at the sensation of being emerged in a place he fully didn't belong.

Why now? he asked.

But deep down, he knew the answer. Lynn.

Jayden wanted to think that Damien had taken residence inside of him again, but he hadn't been alive when the hospital was in full operation. Jayden looked down at his hands, studied how delicate they were, and had the sudden feeling that Victoria had gotten her hands on him this time.

He didn't fight her. He let her guide him. Across the room, a door led to a medical supply closet filled with shelves that held everything from gauze to bandages to syringes. Jayden slammed back into his own body, and his vision went black. When he regained himself, he realized he'd made it back to Lynn's side. Jayden glanced in the direction of the closet.

"I'm gonna fix this," he promised Lynn, and stood up. He swiped her lighter from among the debris and clicked it to life.

The tiny bit of light didn't help much. It exaggerated the wound on Lynn's face, making her look gaunter and frailer. The pile they had built looked rougher too. A fresh wave of guilt swept over him again. Jayden did his best to stave off the self-pity and hurried to where the room should've been.

In the present, it was sealed off by a huge mound of bricks and debris.

"Shit," he said and stuck his fingers in his hair, making it stand up at all angles as he considered what to do next.

Lynn wouldn't give up.

He started to throw the debris to the side, piece by careful piece. Jayden knew he wouldn't be able to move a big wooden beam, but if he could make a gap above or below it, it would be enough for him to squeeze through. Some of the rubble crumbled to ash in his fingers, but most of it remained steady, firm. A flash of pain came as a nail snagged his palm, and he cried out, thinking of all the vaccines he'd have to get when this adventure was all said and done.

His fingertips started to bleed from the rough edges of the wood and stone, but he managed to create a hole large enough to squeeze through. More blackness lurked on the other side, and Jayden's stomach sloshed as he stared into it.

A portal to Hell.

Crawling from one side of the opening to the other gave him the impression that he was climbing into an abyss. A horrible pit from which he'd never emerge. Musty air threatened to choke him and hordes of spiderwebs covered every inch of space. He clicked on the lighter again, watching as one of them sizzled away to nothing.

The inside of the closet didn't look much better than the rest of the basement. The fire had scattered debris in here too, the shelves broken, and the hordes of supplies scattered in every direction. Jayden was glad to see that there *were* still supplies. Part of him worried they'd be gone for some reason or the other.

Jayden gathered up all the bandages he could see. He sifted through the other items but didn't know if he'd need any of them. Hopefully, Lynn's wound wouldn't require more than this. He rushed back to her, setting his fingers to the side of her throat, feeling her steady pulse thrum.

"Can you hear me?" he asked.

No response.

Jayden went to work wiping away the blood before he placed a bandage over the worst of the gore. He brushed a strand of hair out of her eyes and pictured her face from the first time he'd seen her inside the ice cream shop.

Something warm stirred him for their proximity, and he jumped at the sensation, unsure if the feelings were his own or Damien's.

Chapter Twenty-Seven
Lynn

LYNN WAS USED to migraines. The medicine that pumped through her veins daily made sure of that. What she *wasn't* used to was this new piercing pain in her skull. It felt as if someone had struck her. Then she remembered the fall, her rough landing, and groaned.

"Lynn! Lynn, can you hear me?"

Jayden.

Lynn struggled to open her eyes. In the blackness, she couldn't see him, but she could *feel* his presence, how close he was to her.

"Yes," she rasped, wincing at the pain in her throat. How long had she been unconscious? "What happened?"

"You hit your head pretty hard," Jayden said. "Some debris fell on top of you too."

Tentatively, she poked the bandages across her forehead. "Where'd you find these?"

"There's a supply closet on the other side of the basement," Jayden replied and scratched behind his ear. "So, uh, how do you feel? Think you can stand?"

"I'm gonna have to, aren't I?" she asked and started shuffling, trying her best to stand. Her hand came down to rest on something solid and slender. When she put enough pressure, it squished.

"What is *that*?" she howled, yanking her hand away from it.

"That would be the doctor."

"What?"

"I-I had another one of those *visions,* and well, it showed me that *he* was the one who started the fire. Except he did too good of a job and stayed longer than he should've. The stairs were covered in flames, and he trapped himself here."

Lynn wiped her hand on her clothes, desperate to get rid of the sensation of the man's skeleton. "That's Karma in action, I suppose." She took a deep breath. "We need to get out of here."

"Agreed," Jayden said. "But this time, I'm going first."

Lynn didn't argue. She groaned and stood, following Jayden. They rearranged the mound to give it a more solid foundation, but it didn't help ease Lynn's tension when Jayden started to climb. If he was distressed, he didn't voice it until he made it to the top.

"Oh, my God," he said.

The boards creaked, and Lynn's stomach lurched. If he fell and got hurt, they could both end up with concussions. Jayden clapped his hands together, pepping himself up, and leaped.

Silence, then, "I made it!" There was an edge to his voice as if even he couldn't believe he'd made it. "Your turn."

Lynn didn't move at first. Her head throbbed with the

memory of her original tumble.

You've got this, a soft voice floated through the despair in her head.

Damien.

His voice took away all her fear. She climbed, submitting her worries to a higher power. If Damien was here, was really watching over her, he wouldn't let her get hurt.

Not again anyway.

"I'll catch you," Jayden said though she wondered how he could make such a promise in their current predicament.

She jumped. Her heart fell to her stomach, and she had the sickening thought that she'd underestimated the distance and would fall again. When she started to slide backward, Jayden grabbed her wrists, holding her in mid-air.

"I got ya," he said, gasping as he heaved her up onto the floor beside him.

Lynn crawled forward a few paces until she hit the wall. Certain she was safe, she laid her head on the floor and let her heart slow down. "Thank God that's over."

"Yeah," Jayden said, "but now we're back in the same situation we were in an hour ago."

"I think if we go deeper into the wing, we'll find an exit."

"Why would there be one this way? We haven't found any other one beside the front door so far."

"I don't necessarily mean a door," Lynn said. "If this

wing was the source of the fire, the walls might be weak. Frail. Maybe we can break out."

"Okay," Jayden agreed, but he sounded tired, worn out.

Lynn was too. Silently, she hoped the hall really would lead to an exit. She didn't want to imagine the possibility of spending the night here.

Chapter Twenty-Eight
Jayden

JAYDEN AND LYNN walked for what felt like hours, but there were no breaks in the wall that Jayden could see. The walls were made of brick and mortar, most of them holding strong. Jayden tapped it every few feet, hoping that Lynn was right, but so far, no luck.

There were no signs of an emergency exit either.

"You think the front door is really the only way in and out?" Jayden asked at last.

"I don't want to think it is. There has to be another way out. A way that they carried bodies out without the public seeing."

"Maybe they did it in plain view."

The path they walked eventually looped back to the lobby. Jayden tested the doors again, and Lynn stood nearby, watching as if she wanted to spare herself the pain of false hope.

Jayden pushed and pulled, the doors rattling, but they didn't budge.

"No luck?"

"No luck."

"So now what?" she asked. "There's no food or water here. If we're going to be here for a while, we need to find supplies."

Jayden sniffled with the smell of ash in his nostrils. Any food or water that had been in the place would've spoiled long ago. "We're screwed by the sounds of it."

Lynn buried her face in her hands before peering up at him. "We should take some time to rest and get our strength back up."

"You're not supposed to sleep with a concussion," Jayden said, staring at her mess of curls.

"I don't have a concussion," she murmured. "Besides, the whole *'don't sleep with a concussion'* thing is a myth. You gotta wake the person every thirty minutes or so, and it's fine."

"I'm not gonna risk it. Besides, what about that monster or whatever it is?"

"We haven't heard it in a little while. Maybe it'll leave us alone since we found all the secrets in this place."

If only things were so easy.

"Why don't we try the windows? There are bars, but they're old and rusty. They might break."

"Better than nothing."

Jayden stared at the nearest window, looking for anything that seemed odd or out of place. The window sat level to his shoulders, a tiny beam of moonlight streaming in. Jayden grabbed the bars and pulled.

"It's gonna be a miracle if I don't get tetanus from all this," he said when one of the cuts on his palm touched the rust.

Lynn stood back, watching, and Jayden braced

himself. He jerked his arms, trying to loosen the bars. His muscles quivered, and he gritted his teeth, feeling some of the resistance give way.

"They're coming loose," he said, hope pulsing through him for the first time in hours.

A roar in the distance made the hair on the back of his neck stand up. He glanced over his shoulder, pulling harder and harder as the sound drew closer.

"Shit, it's coming," Lynn said. "We have to go!"

Jayden didn't want to move. The bars were almost free. A little more time and they could be separated from the wall completely.

Lynn let out a piercing shriek that shook Jayden to the core as the first bar came free. He looked over his shoulder, and his vision went white. A giant swirling mass of brightness that filled his heart with dread.

"Jayden! Jayden, help!" Lynn screamed, but Jayden could hardly grasp the situation unfolding around him.

In the thick haze, he couldn't see her. "Where are you?" he howled, rushing forward as the fog started to dissipate. All at once, it vanished, and the hall plunged into darkness.

Lynn had gone with it.

Despair crept across Jayden's skin like spiders, and all he could do was think of Kasey and Kay. One missing and one dead. The thought of Lynn sharing either of their fate made him ache. Steadily the ache turned to anger.

He could imagine that the monster, demon, or

whatever it may be was really all that remained of the terrible doctor who had spent his entire life inflicting pain on others, specifically girls like Lynn. He deserved to suffer for everything he'd done, and Jayden was going to make sure that happened, even if he died trying.

He turned to go back and the lighter blinked out. Frustrated, he tried to ignite it again, and his foot thudded into something. Not expecting the force, he toppled forward. A crash and a thud came as something shattered. The stink of chemicals drifted up his nose, and he realized a second too late what it was—the stink of a kerosene lanturn.

Flames blossomed up with a great roar. At first, the fire crackled, but nothing happened. One tiny flame defied the others and leaped to a wooden beam, making a home there. It grew larger and larger, embers dripping to the floor. In a flash, the fire nearly surrounded him. He stood there, staring at what he'd done, a haunting reminder that he'd limited the time they had to escape.

Chapter Twenty-Nine
Lynn

WHEN THE WHITE haze surrounded Lynn, she thought she was a goner. She thought of Jayden's friend and tried to imagine how much pain she was about to endure. To her surprise, the mist caused her no discomfort. It eased it *away,* luring her into a false sense of serenity that left her incredibly tired. Despite the voices in her head screaming that she shouldn't give in, she did.

Her mind filled with images of her and Damien— dates they'd gone on while holding hands and eating ice cream, visions of them lying in flowery meadows and pointing up to the clouds. Her heart ached with desire, and as the memory drew to a close, her fight drifted away.

She belonged here. At Damien's side.

This is why I was lured to the asylum.

It had been Damien's way of drawing her back to him.

Lynn's vision started to go black, and she was ready to let it take her away when pain radiated from the spot in her temple where she'd hit her head. It was sharp and new as if she'd injured herself all over again. Gasping, she came back to consciousness, vision black with the shadows inside the asylum.

She blinked, feeling out her surroundings. She was

sitting on something—a chair? When she tried to move her wrists and ankles, she realized they were bound. Turning her head, she tried to see who or what else was in the room with her.

"Jayden?" she tried to say, only to realize a cloth gag blocked her mouth.

Alarm bells went off, some so loud her ears started to ring. A soft voice whispered, *You're going to be alright.*

It was Victoria. She didn't know why her voice comforted her, but it did. What was *alright* to a ghost anyway?

"I bet you're confused," a voice drifted from the shadows, and Lynn froze.

She'd assumed she was alone. She squinted, trying once again to see whoever lurked in the shadows. She'd assumed she was in another flashback, a horrible memory of Victoria's, but something about this was different. *Realer* somehow.

In the visions, half the man's face had been covered with a mask, but this man's wasn't. The curve of his jaw and the shadow over his eyes stood out. He looked young. Far younger than a doctor could be…right?

"I picked this room on purpose," the man said as if he'd read her thoughts. "I think part of the fear comes from the not knowing, wouldn't you agree?"

"*Who are you?*" Lynn tried to ask around the gag.

"Ah, let me get that for you," the man said, and a cold finger traced her lips as he pulled the gag loose.

"I asked who you are," Lynn snarled the second her mouth was free. The voice sounded different too.

"I don't think it really benefits you to know, does it? Though I have to say part of you must already have some clue."

The gears in Lynn's brain started to turn. If the thing pursuing them was a ghost, or a demon, they could possess a body. Perhaps the body of Jayden's missing friend? "You're the doctor."

"One smart cookie," he said, waggling a finger at her. "One smart cookie indeed."

"So what do you want with me?"

"The same thing I wanted with all those pretty little crazy girls," he said with a deep, throaty laugh.

The sound sent chills right down Lynn's spine. "You tortured her. Victoria...she lived in fear of you."

"Is that right? I've never seen it," he said. "I would've been a bit softer on her if she would've shown that fear instead of always bearing her teeth, pretending to be so much stronger than she actually was."

"What? You think because she heard voices that she was some sort of damsel in distress? You have no *idea* what kind of character builder it is to question your own sanity daily. She *was* strong, and so am I."

He stared at her through half-lidded eyes. "You're starting to bore me, my dear."

Lynn listened to his footsteps as he moved farther away. Metal clanked on metal as something shifted, and

Lynn was reminded of the tiny tools a dentist would pick up and put down while working on her teeth.

"What are you doing?" she demanded.

"What I do best."

She heard shuffling sounds as he came closer, and Lynn caught sight of a slender object in his hand when a dim beam of moonlight reflected off it. A scalpel. Lynn thought of the mutilated body in the day room and fought viciously against her binds.

"Where to begin," the man mused, placing the cold metal to the side of her throat. She stiffened, and he moved it, tapping it to the top of her arm and then the side of her leg.

Lynn didn't even breathe as she waited for the blade to sink through her flesh. She gritted her teeth, and at last, he pulled the scalpel away. He laughed, and Lynn's shoulders drooped. He was toying with her, doing what he could to break her mind *and* body.

The clatter of footsteps as he crossed the room came again, and he tossed the scalpel onto the tray with a tiny *clink.* "You know, you look like her," the doctor said as he rummaged through his stuff. "Victoria."

Lynn pulled against her binds, angrier than she'd been earlier. "You don't have a right to talk about her. Not after what you did. Not after you left her to die in that fire."

"She got her revenge," he snarled. "Don't forget, *I* died in the fire too."

"You get what you deserve."

"It's easy to judge a situation when you don't have the full picture."

"I don't need a full picture to know you're insane," Lynn said, licking away the spit that gathered in the corners of her mouth. "That you got off on torturing people who weren't able to defend themselves."

"Don't you know how impossible my job was?" he asked, voice going weak and quiet. "People brought me their sick, crazy family members, and I was expected to cure them. But guess what? There *is* no cure for people like that. They lived in misery. They were *grateful* to be freed from that life."

Lynn went cold. "You think you did them a favor by murdering them?"

"I know I did."

"That's bullshit. Mental illnesses will never be easy to live with, but I can't imagine all those people lining up for your *mercy*."

"Look me in the eyes and tell me you wouldn't rather be dead. That you wouldn't jump at the opportunity to be reunited with your lost love. He's here too, you know. Has been and always will be."

Lynn's eyes welled with tears. "Keep him out of your mouth."

"You haven't told me I'm wrong."

Lynn bit her lip to keep from snarling. Of course she'd do anything to be with Damien again. *Except give this monster the satisfaction of knowing he's right.*

"You killed him, didn't you." She meant it as a question, but it came out cold, flat, devoid of emotion. She didn't need to ask because deep down, part of her already knew. The creature she'd heard storming the halls had appeared in the woods, and in the resulting chaos, Damien had been killed.

Makes far more sense than a hunting accident ever could.

Lynn pulled against the ropes, screaming out as she tried to pull herself free. "You better hope you kill me before I make it out of this. When I get my hands on you, you're gonna wish you stayed dead."

The doctor lifted his chin and peered down his nose at her. It gave him a hawkish appearance, morphing his face into something that wasn't altogether human. "It's gonna be so much more fun to kill you now that you know the truth."

He took a step forward, and Lynn focused on the silver clamp in his hand. Before he reached her, he stopped, staring straight ahead as if a great beast lurked behind her. Something he dared not approach. A hazy white glow appeared around him, reminding Lynn of the light from a UFO. In the places where the white touched him, he started to smoke. Rolls of bright orange fire tore through him, and he screamed, trying to put it out.

The fire ravished him, reducing him to a thing rather than a human. The screaming stopped, and the shadowy outline of his body thumped to the floor at her feet. Lynn craned her neck to stare at it, waiting for it to move. When it didn't, she sagged in relief. Wherever Jayden had gone, he hadn't forgotten her. Hadn't forgotten their mission.

You did it, Jayden.

Chapter Thirty
Jayden

A SHARP PIERCING wail echoed down the hallway and reverberated down Jayden's spine. He recognized that sound. Those were Lynn's screams.

He didn't expect to make it far, but somehow, he sprinted down the hall with ease as if someone else had taken control of him. Jayden let go of his fear as he approached the awful room where he'd found the remains of his friend. He wanted to stop, to go a different direction, to avoid that room altogether.

If he was a coward, the task would be simple.

But he wasn't, and so the situation was made harder by his morality. He had a chance to save Lynn from sharing Kay's fate, and so he'd face the worst to make it happen.

Plunging through the last few feet, he rounded the corner, stopping when he saw Lynn in a tiny trickle of moonlight. She'd been bound to a chair, face frazzled as she tried to pull herself free of the restraints. Relief breezed through him for only a second until he realized she wasn't alone. A man lay on the floor beside her, groaning as he struggled to pull himself up.

At first, Jayden was convinced it was an intruder, the real person who'd been behind Kay's death, when he realized something else instead.

"Kasey!" he cried, wrapping his arms around his friend. He squeezed until Kasey's breath came out in a strained huff.

"Jayden?" he asked at last before he returned the hug, awkwardly wrapping his arms around Jayden's ribs.

"Yeah, buddy, it's me."

"Jayden?" Lynn's soft voice called.

Remembering the reason for his quest, Jayden rose on shaky legs and approached.

"I'm here," he said and went to work loosening her bonds. He couldn't see any new injuries and prayed she had no new psychological ones as well. "Are you okay?"

She bobbed her head and stood up, grasping his shoulder for leverage. "You know this fucker?"

Jayden tossed an arm over her shoulder, helping her stay steady though he suspected she could've managed on her own. "He's my friend," Jayden said then paled at the realization of what had happened. *Kasey* had been the one responsible for this. "The one I was looking for," he added and tried to drop to the ground beside him, but Lynn halted, not wanting to get closer.

Jayden let go of her and knelt beside his friend. "What happened to you? I really thought you were dead."

Kasey sat up enough to lean his back against the wall and check his legs for injuries. "I-I don't remember much of anything to tell you the truth. One minute, we were driving, and the next, the car stopped working. I wanted to fix it, but the rain started. I told Kay I'd walk up the road to a payphone and then I heard someone calling me from the woods."

"Kay too?"

"I don't know," Kasey said, eyes two shining pools. "It's all a haze. I was there, and now I'm here with you two. Is Kay..."

Lynn and Jayden exchanged uncertain glances, feeling the warmth dwindle away. They'd made it this far, but there was no easy way to wrap their brains around the fact that not everyone had been so fortunate.

"S-she's dead," Jayden said. He didn't know how he'd explain the inevitable follow-up question *How'd it happen?* He wasn't sure how anything in the past few hours of his life had happened.

Lynn looked away as if she feared she'd have to be the one to carry the conversation.

"She died here," Kasey said flatly.

Jayden's heart pounded, his mind alight with the memories of finding her body. He hoped her remains were far enough in the shadows that he'd avoid getting another glimpse.

The next question out of Kasey's mouth hadn't been what Jayden expected.

"Did I do it? Did I kill her?"

Jayden blinked a few times, trying to compose himself. "I-I don't know," he said at last, trying to sound supportive, comforting, and not as if he was on the verge of losing his mind. "Did you see things?"

Kasey looked down, and Jayden could feel Lynn's

scorching glare burning a hole in the side of his face. "If you did, know it wasn't really you who did it. The spirits possessed you."

Kasey's face drew tight. "I-I have these memories. A lot of...images. How do I know I didn't do it?"

"Because we all heard voices," Lynn said. "You're not alone."

Kasey peered up at her, eyes narrowed, as if he didn't believe her. Didn't want to make eye contact with the second girl he'd almost murdered in cold blood.

Jayden glanced at her, wondering if she'd mention the fact that she'd heard voices *before* this had all began.

"What did they say to you?" Kasey asked in a soft whisper.

"They guided us here, to you," Jayden said.

"And now we're all together."

Jayden breathed in and picked up the smell of smoke. A strangling sensation choked him when he remembered the fire he'd lit. The situation he'd put them in.

"And now we need to get the hell out of here."

Chapter Thirty-One
Lynn

LYNN COULD HARDLY catch her breath. It seemed nothing short of ironic that after everything, they'd risk death by fire. She couldn't see it yet, but she'd swear the slightest hint of smoke lingered in her nostrils.

"What did you do?" she asked, eyes shining.

"I tripped on one of those kerosene lanterns, and it broke. Let's just say it and my lighter didn't get along too well."

Lynn grunted. "Do you remember where the window was?"

"There's no time to get back to it," Jayden said, frustrated for the fact he'd put them in this predicament.

"There's a back door," Kasey piped up, causing them both to stop.

"That's impossible. We searched the entire hospital."

"I don't think the doctor wanted anyone to know about it," Kasey said, clearly uncomfortable that he knew this bit of information that they didn't. "It was in his office. This secret little place he had built for himself."

Lynn sighed, deep and long. "Of course. From what we know about him, that seems right for his character. How do we get to it?"

Kasey scrunched his face, looking as if he'd be

violently ill. "I can...*sort* of remember, but without him guiding me, I'm not one hundred percent sure."

"You'll figure it out on the way."

They hurried down the hall, Jayden and Lynn a pace behind Kasey.

Lynn didn't look at Jayden as she said, "I didn't get a chance to thank you for saving my life."

"It was the least I could do," he said quickly. Perhaps a little *too* quickly. She wondered if he was thinking of the incident in the basement again.

Kasey took a sharp left, and Lynn almost skidded to a halt. When he'd mentioned an exit, she assumed it would be on the other side of the asylum. Instead, he'd taken a path leading *toward* the fire.

"We can't go this way, man," Jayden said, sounding as frightened as Lynn felt.

"But it's the way," Kasey insisted.

Jayden cringed, and Lynn could almost identify all the emotions mixed into it. "Okay."

This is a terrible idea, Lynn thought over and over.

If Kasey was right, if this *was* the only other way out, they'd have to risk it. The air started to get hotter, flames audibly crackling, and Lynn stopped.

"The fire's too close. We have to turn around."

"No! Just a little more," Kasey insisted. "We're almost there."

Jayden and Lynn exchanged an exasperated glare, but they trudged onward, zigzagging down another hallway.

Flames crackled at the end of it.

Lynn held a sleeve over her face and nose, coughing as the smoke gagged her. Debris started to rain from the ceiling, and Lynn had the horrific thought that the entire roof would cave in and kill all three of them. A corridor branched into another hallway, and Kasey bolted down it.

"Not much farther now!" he hollered over his shoulder.

"He's gonna get us all killed," Lynn said. She glanced over her shoulder, missing the cool stale air of the rest of the hospital.

This air was hot. Too hot. It breezed over her skin and caused the slightest bit of sweat to dew on her temples. The hallway narrowed until only one of them could fit at a time. Jayden went first, followed by Lynn. Kasey was last to follow when a flaming chunk of wood fell from the roof, blocking the hall.

At first, no one moved. No one *could* move. The door was only a few feet away for her and Jayden but for Kasey? He tried to get over the beam once, but the space left between it and the wall was small, the space easily full of flames.

Teary-eyed, he said, "I can't go with you."

"That's nonsense, man, we can—" Jayden tried to argue.

"There's no time," Kasey said.

A creak from the roof overhead punctuated his point.

"You guys have to go."

"I can't leave you here."

Kasey gave him a small, bitter smile and turned, running *back* down the hall in the direction they'd come from.

"Kasey! Don't do this!" Jayden hollered after him.

Lynn looked between him and the door, listening to the creak overhead intensify. Out of options, she grabbed his arm, pulling him in the direction of freedom. "We have to go!"

Jayden didn't move at first. Then he looked at her. When their eyes met, something broke in him, and he went with her. Together, they busted through the door. Fresh air breezed up her nose, and Lynn hurried faster, tumbling out into the wet grass beside Jayden. Both of them broke into a coughing fit, Lynn's eyes streaming water as the cold night air cooled her down.

She pulled herself backward, as far from the building as she could. Sweet air filled her lungs, and she forced herself to breathe, to get rid of all the bad things she'd inhaled. Jayden hunched beside her, hands on his upper thighs as ragged breaths tore through his chest, the sounds a mix of sobs and gasping for air.

A sound that would've hurt her soul if she hadn't been so freaked out by everything already. Lynn looked up at the roof of the asylum, watching the visible flames roar toward the sky. She thought of Victoria's tiny skeleton nestled inside the bathtub and Kasey running through the halls and sent up a silent prayer.

Let you be free at last, she thought, staring at the stars overhead that seemed the slightest bit brighter.

Thank you, Victoria's soft voice replied.

In spite of everything, a smile crossed Lynn's face. She hugged herself as Jayden plopped down beside her, watching the flames. They didn't speak as the blaze grew stronger and stronger.

They'd done a good thing.

Now, Lynn was ready to escape, to get back home into the arms of her overprotective sister and mother. No doubt they were worried about her and had spent the last few hours searching madly for her.

"I think it's time to go home," Lynn said.

Jayden looked at her, firelight reflecting the tears in his eyes. "I know."

They didn't speak again as they walked into the trees. The light from the fire made the first half of the journey considerably easier than Lynn had thought it would be. For the other half, she and Jayden called to one another, making sure they didn't wander too far apart in the shadows. Lynn didn't let herself think about the voices that had lured them out here to begin with.

Eventually, they stumbled onto the road. Kasey's car glinted in the moonlight, the devastated remains of Jayden's not too far away.

"What do we do now?" Jayden asked, so absolutely exhausted that even thinking seemed too hard.

"We need to go to the police. Tell them all that's happened." Jayden didn't mention Kay, but Lynn knew it was what they both thought about.

"Let's get back to my house," Lynn suggested. "We can get some food, rest, and then figure it out."

Jayden halted. "*Figure it out*? My friends are dead!"

Lynn gave him a small bitter smile but responded as if she hadn't heard him speak. "It's about a mile down the road."

"Fine." Jayden stormed past her, and Lynn trailed behind. Softly, she said, "I need you to do me a favor when we get there."

Jayden raised an eyebrow, peering at her uncertainly.

"My mom and sister...they think I'm nuts. That I can't function on my own. When I tell them what's happened, where I've been, they're never going to believe me. They're going to think... They're going to think I'm getting worse. They might try to get me committed. Can you just...be there when I tell them? Tell them I'm not crazy?

Jayden didn't say anything for a long minute, so long that Lynn was certain he was thinking of the perfect way to let her down. At last, he said, "I can do that for you."

"Thank you," Lynn said, though she hadn't ruled out the possibility that she *was* crazy after all.

Chapter Thirty-Two
Jayden

LYNN'S HOUSE WAS a small, cozy little thing pushed back a ways from the road. It was almost completely surrounded by trees, and Jayden tried to imagine what it would've been like growing up here. It must've been quiet.

What does that kind of silence do to a person?

Jayden needed the noise of the city, the sound of other people in the distance to let him know he wasn't alone. Out here? Who's to say.

By the time Jayden made it to the base of the stairs, Lynn was already pulling open the door. A blonde girl who looked similar to Lynn stood beyond the frame, staring at them. She rushed toward Lynn, planting a kiss to her forehead before she pulled her into a hug.

"Oh, my God, Lynn!" she was saying. "I was so worried when you didn't come back, and then I *found* your medicine by the road and thought something terrible had happened." She pulled away sharply. "Don't *ever* scare me like that again!" Then she noticed Jayden and froze. "Oh, hello."

Lynn glanced toward him. In the dim porchlight, he could see her better than he'd been able to during most of their adventure. On instinct, his eyes traveled up to the bandage under her hairline. It was brown with old blood, and he wondered how long it would be until her sister noticed it.

"Amelia, this is Jayden. I...have a story to tell you, and I feared you wouldn't believe me."

Amelia's face eased slightly. "Yes, of course. Come on in out of the cold."

At first, Jayden had had the irrational fear that this woman would turn them away. As he stepped inside, he felt a bit better. Knitted blankets hung across the back of the green couch, and a bright red rug sat in the middle of the hardwood floor.

Amelia sank into the armchair beside the couch, and Lynn stood between them all if she was afraid of sitting down and putting an actual end to their adventure.

Amelia glared at Lynn through half-lidded eyes. "Where've you been? Mom cried herself to sleep not an hour ago." Her eyes moved to the bandage on her forehead. "And what happened to your head?"

Jayden could see the hesitation on her face before she said, "It's a long story."

"Let's get you cleaned up," Amelia said and dragged Lynn out of the room. Before they disappeared, Lynn paused to look over her shoulder. "Be right back."

Jayden let himself relax into the couch, thinking of all that had happened. He could still remember the residual feeling after Damien and Victoria had possessed him. It wasn't a good feeling.

The more he thought about it, the worse he felt about their entire future. In the woods, it had been easy to imagine that they'd explain what had happened to Kay and Kasey. Now he doubted it would be so simple.

Lynn came back, clean bandages on her forehead, and her face clean of dirt.

"Okay. I need y'all to spill your story," Amelia said, setting her hands on her hips as Lynn made her way to Jayden's side.

Lynn stared him down, just as afraid as he was, except in her case, she didn't fear the police. She feared her sister.

That's why I'm here, he wanted to tell her and hoped his eyes said as much.

Lynn took a breath and turned toward her sister. "You remember when my ears started bleeding yesterday?"

"Vividly," Amelia said, blinking quickly.

"What I didn't tell you was the voices I heard. Ones that weren't my own. One of them...one of them told me to come find it."

Amelia drew her eyebrows together, instantly concerned. "You're hearing new voices?"

Lynn plopped down on the couch beside Jayden. "Yes. I did. At first...at first, I thought it might only be me. I ignored it. Then I had a nightmare, and I heard the voice there too. When I left earlier to go for a walk, the voice called from the woods again. So I...followed it."

"That's so irresponsible!" Amelia gushed. Her cheeks flushed red, and Jayden stiffened, uncomfortable with being caught in the middle of such a heated conversation.

"I mean no disrespect, Ma'am," he cut in. "But we *all* heard voices today."

Amelia's sharp glare turned to him. He didn't flinch, but he could tell she thought he was lying.

"It started raining," Lynn said, trying to diffuse some of the tension. "There was lightning too. I remembered in school that you're not supposed to stand near trees in case one gets struck so I thought my best bet was to get out of the woods. Except I got turned around and ended up going deeper into the woods instead of out to the road. I found shelter in this old building."

Amelia's eyes closed as she said, "West Gate Hospital."

"You're heard of it?" Jayden asked.

Amelia's eyes fluttered back open. "There are lots of rumors about the place. None of them good."

"Has anyone been there since it was shut down?"

"Who's to say? It's not as if they put anything up to keep people out."

"Yeah, we noticed," Lynn grumbled.

"So how'd you meet then?" Amelia asked, raising an eyebrow.

"I was separated from my friends," Jayden said. "You probably already know this, but me and them came here for the touristy stuff yesterday. I was their…third wheel so ditching me was something they did pretty often. This time though, something was wrong. I had this bad feeling in my gut, and I had a dream telling me they were in danger. I tried to drive back to town when I found my friend's car abandoned on the side of the road. I went into the woods looking for him and ended up at the hospital."

"We bumped into each other not too long after that," Lynn said.

Jayden peered at Lynn from the corner of his eye, sensing a theme. They were spoon-feeding her sister this story by dialing down the crazy. He could understand that, but at the same time, he didn't want to do it. What had happened to them *was* crazy, it *was* hard to believe, but it had happened.

"We sort of…set it on fire," Lynn admitted.

Amelia puffed her cheeks, not speaking for a long time. When she finally let the air out, she said, "I guess all I can say is that at least no one was seriously injured."

Jayden and Lynn exchanged a long look of knowing despair. They hadn't discussed this part and only too late realized the error of their ways. Jayden could tell Lynn wouldn't be the one to speak. To decide how they proceeded from here. That was on his shoulders.

"Yeah," he said softly.

Lynn pushed her lips together in a tight expression.

Amelia looked between Lynn and Jayden. Jayden wondered if she'd caught the look between them, and if she wondered what it meant when she said, "I think you two should get some sleep."

Chapter Thirty-Three
Lynn

"I CAN'T BELIEVE it's actually over," Jayden said, breaking Lynn out of her trance as they traveled down the hall together.

"Me too," Lynn said and gestured to the first room they passed. "Amelia said to tell you she left some clothes on the bathroom sink for you."

"Thanks," Jayden said. "How's your head?"

Lynn patted the fresh bandages Amelia had put there. "Not bad. Amelia said I'm clear of a concussion."

"That's something," Jayden said, shuffling his foot as the conversation went awkwardly silent. Without imminent danger threatening to close in on them, it was as if they suddenly didn't know how to be around one another.

"I think I'm going to get a shower in," he said awkward and took a step toward the room.

Softly, she said, "Hey."

He stopped to look at her.

"Thank you again for well...everything," she said and looked down at the ground. "I don't know how many doctor appointments and therapy sessions you've saved me from."

"I wouldn't rule out the therapy sessions yet," Jayden said. When Lynn narrowed her eyes at him, he added, "I think after all that's happened, we could *all* use some therapy."

"You're not kidding."

"G'night."

"Good night."

Her bedroom was a few doors down from the bathroom, so she held back, waiting until she heard the sound of the bathroom door closing before she closed her own door. She listened to the sounds of running water as she changed into her pajamas and settled into bed, grateful for the feel of her familiar surroundings. Lynn turned onto her side, staring at the shadows on the wall. Her head began to throb with the onset of another migraine, and she lifted her fingers to touch the bandage, convinced it was more in her head than an actual symptom.

I need to sleep, she reasoned.

For all the terrible things she'd seen in the asylum, it was surprisingly easy to fall asleep. When her eyes fluttered open, she was in the clearing beside the hospital, and her stomach lurched, making her sick. Had the entire experience of the day been nothing more than the product of her mind? She opened her mouth to scream when a voice called to her, stopping her.

"Hey, pumpkin pie," Damien's voice lilted through her mind.

Her tears dried as she turned to face him. He stood at the edge of the trees, long black hair moving subtly in the wind. A smile touched his lips, and as she watched, he lifted his arms, gesturing for her to approach. Lynn threw herself at him, breathing in his scent. After all this time, she'd almost forgotten what he smelled like. He felt so solid, so real, that she didn't want to let go.

Some part of her brain knew what would happen when she did, and she didn't want that to be her reality. She wanted to live in this moment forever.

Damien's fingers grasped the tops of her shoulders, fingers massaging her gently as he held her at arm's length, staring at her. "I came to say goodbye," he said, eyes boring into hers.

Lynn's heart felt as if it were ready to break all over again. "But why, Damien? You could take me with you."

Damien smiled, one cold finger wiping away a tear that gathered beneath her large eyes. "If I could, I would, but it wouldn't be right. You still have the chance to live a long life. Live it well and blessed. I'll be here for you when your time comes."

"It's not fair," Lynn choked out. "My life was supposed to be with *you*. What's the point knowing that I'm alone?"

"Remember the cliché saying?" Damien asked and set the tip of his finger to the place above Lynn's heart. "You're not alone because I'm always in here. Every time your heart beats, it's me encouraging you to live. When you find someone who makes your heart race—" Lynn opened her mouth to protest but Damien continued to speak, not giving her the chance to interrupt "—when you find that person, you will remember the way that your heart used to beat for me, and you will know that it's time to move on."

Thick salty tears started to stream down Lynn's cheeks, and she didn't stop them. It didn't matter how much she didn't want him to go because he was already gone. All the crying in the world wouldn't bring him back. At the very least, she'd have a gift that not many other people in her situation got—the chance to say goodbye.

Chapter Thirty-Four
Jayden

JAYDEN WOKE IN the morning with a snort. He sat straight up, the early rays of dawn filtering over him. It took a minute for him to remember where he was. Voices and the sound of clattering plates came from downstairs, and on instinct, he followed it. Amelia, Lynn, and the woman he presumed to be their mother were there, setting the table for breakfast.

Amelia looked up as Jayden entered. "Just in time."

Jayden bobbed his head, uncertainly sitting in the chair nearest him. He wasn't used to family meals, having a place set for him, but he didn't want to make them uncomfortable by making that much apparent.

"How'd you sleep?" Lynn asked, plopping into the chair next to him.

He stared at her, at her rumpled hair and the bags under her eyes. It didn't look as if she'd slept particularly well, and the fact that she was awake so much sooner than he had been supported his theory.

"Good," he said as the woman piled food onto his plate. He stared at it, mouth-watering, and offered her a pleasant smile.

"We didn't get to talk last night," she said to him as she circled the table, setting the pan back on the stove.

"No, we didn't. I'm sorry about that *Ms.*?"

"Oh, polite this one," she said, smiling at Lynn.

Lynn stared down at her plate, pretending not to notice.

"I'm Jayden," he said, extending a hand.

Lynn's mother smiled. "I'm Catherine. You can call me Cat. Don't worry about the *Ms.* stuff. I'm not that old."

"Right," Jayden said, laughing, and plopped a bite of food into his mouth.

Catherine sat down across from him. "Oh, Lord, we thank you for this food," she began.

Jayden stopped chewing midbite, panic making his eyes wide. The last thing he wanted was to insult these women after everything they'd done. Lynn looked at him with a similar expression on her face, and suddenly, he felt better.

"Amen," Catherine finished.

Jayden finished chewing, trying to swallow as subtly as possible. He peered across the table to Lynn, wondering what she was thinking.

"Well, this has been great. Thanks for breakfast, Mom," Lynn said and pushed away from the table suddenly.

"You didn't eat!" Catherine called.

Her plate was barely touched, and Jayden raised an eyebrow, watching her. Lynn cast a glance at Amelia before she left the room, and a minute later, Amelia followed. Uncertainty, Jayden glanced over his shoulder and took another bite before he followed them.

"Well, that's not suspicious at all," Catherine's voice followed him, but he didn't turn to look at her.

"What is it?" Lynn asked her sister as Jayden slipped into the room with them.

Amelia turned at the sound of his footsteps, relaxing after she realized it wasn't Catherine. "No one knows about the hospital as far as I can tell. I think your best bet is to pretend you were never there, and no one will ever know it was you guys."

Jayden opened his mouth and closed it again.

Lynn frowned. "Are you going to be able to do that?"

He wanted to say *yes,* to act as if everything would be okay, but it could never truly be okay again. When he went home, he would have to acknowledge the fact that his friends were missing.

People would ask questions, and he ached at the thought of their families.

He held his eyes closed for a long time before he said, "Yeah."

Amelia puffed her cheeks. "I hate this. I really do, but I feel like—" She paused to look away before looking back at Jayden and Lynn. "—I'm worried there's something I don't know."

"Like what?" Lynn asked, clearly offended. Jayden was almost put out by how easily she hid their secret.

Amelia blinked. "This entire situation isn't you. Seems like someone's been a bad influence." She glanced up at Jayden through her lashes.

He recoiled. He was a lot of things—a liar, a third wheel, an opportunist—but this? Never.

"Why would you say that?" he asked at last. "You don't know anything about me." His heart started to pound as he thought about the situation from her point of view. She wanted to protect her sister. That was what the bottom line was. She would throw him under the bus if she had to. When word of the fire reached town, there *would* be an investigation of sorts. If Kay and Kasey would be found, he couldn't say.

He felt sick. If everyone pointed the blame at him, what would happen?

I knew I never should've agreed to this trip, he thought bitterly.

"What gives, Sissy?" Lynn said, glaring at Amelia. "This isn't his fault."

Now it was Amelia's turn to look sick. "I know you want to believe that, but you were off your medication, Lynn."

"So that makes me completely unreliable?"

"In this case it could," Amelia said, whirling on her. "Don't you understand that? There is going to be an investigation, and you're the weakest link."

Lynn recoiled. "Geez, tell me what you really think."

"No, it's not like that, it's—" She stopped to cover her face with her hands, and Jayden didn't know what to do.

It took him a minute to realize that what was happening wasn't his fault or Lynn's. It was the five stages of grief playing out before his eyes.

"Look, I appreciate you taking me in, but I should go," Jayden said and walked past Amelia and Lynn, sliding his shoes on, all while trying to blink back tears.

Though he wanted to look back, he didn't. It was safer not to.

Chapter Thirty-Five
Lynn

LYNN'S HEAD BUZZED as she tried to process the scene that had played out before her.

"What a power move," Lynn said, unable to feel any warmth for her sister.

Amelia dropped her hands from her eyes, the little bit of wetness that had leaked free smeared her mascara, making her eyes appear even bigger. "What?"

"Blaming Jayden? He's a good guy. What happened wasn't his fault. It wasn't *any* of our faults," Lynn said and hurried away from her sister, desperate to catch Jayden before he was gone for good.

"Lynn, wait!" Amelia called.

"We'll talk later," Lynn replied as the door slammed shut behind her.

That was a conversation she wasn't looking forward to. Not one bit.

"Jayden!" she called.

He stopped mid-step, hand on top of the porch railing. His eyes drooped as he looked at her as if he expected her to hurl more accusations at him.

"I'm sorry," she said, breathless as she reached his side. "For what she said."

"Not your fault," Jayden said, hurrying down the

stairs.

"Yeah, but the way you looked at me in there tells me you blame me somewhat," she said.

Jayden stared straight ahead, not saying a word.

"Well, *I* don't blame you for what happened. And I don't blame Kasey. What we went through is something that will bond us for life, so I hope you don't go home hating me after all this. And if you do, I understand, but know I'm not going to let Amelia hurt you in anyway. She's stressed. Her entire life, she's been this perfect girl, living this perfect life. I think this is the worst thing she's ever experienced, and she doesn't know how to handle it."

Jayden raked his fingers through his hair. "I think it's time for me to get out of here. Get back home and face the music."

Lynn's lip trembled at the thought of saying goodbye. She'd known it was coming, of course, but now that it was here, she hated it. After Damien's death, Lynn had gotten herself accustomed to being alone. His company was the only company over her own that she had enjoyed in a long time, and she didn't want to give that up. She wished she could think up an excuse that would make him stay a little while longer but after Amelia's stunt, she didn't see it happening.

"Take care of yourself," she said, and her voice cracked.

Jayden turned to look at her then, a glaze over his eyes that made her wonder if he'd thought the same thing.

"Maybe we'll meet again one day."

Lynn folded her arms across her chest, staring off into the woods as she tried to gather her thoughts. She supposed it was possible though highly unlikely.

Jayden simpered as if her response hadn't been what he was hoping for. He started to walk down the road, and Lynn stared at the back of his head. After he was gone, crushing loneliness came back to her. Though he'd been a stranger, he knew much more about her than anyone in the world besides her family. With the hollow spot in her chest, she didn't think herself capable of going inside and facing Amelia.

Not yet.

Instead, she plopped down on the bottom porch step, in the same place she used to sit during lazy afternoons with Damien. Tears continued to streak down her face, and she tried to talk herself out of her feelings, to remind herself how ridiculous it was to cry now after everything, but she couldn't help it.

The door behind her clanged open, and she winced.

"You let him leave?" Amelia asked.

"What else could I do?" Lynn asked, hurrying to dry her face on her sleeve though she was already one hundred percent sure Amelia had heard her crying.

"You could've told him to stay."

"Coming from the woman who said he's a bad influence."

Amelia huffed through her nose. "I didn't mean it like

that I...I'm scared. I actually came out here to try and apologize, but I guess it's too late."

Lynn rested her chin on her arm and huffed. "You can say that again."

"Try and imagine this situation from my point of view. What was I supposed to think or do? I want to protect you."

"And you could've done that by believing me. Believing us."

Amelia stared across the road, and Lynn didn't need her to speak to know she'd never believe any of the things Lynn had to say. Her pride wouldn't let her.

"Besides, he doesn't need me holding him back," Lynn said, curling her fingers into her sleeves.

Amelia stepped down the stairs, plopping down beside Lynn. "He didn't act like you held him back."

"You don't need to keep beating a dead horse. He's gone," Lynn said and stood up, brushing leaves and dirt off her before she stormed up the steps and into the house.

Amelia didn't follow her, and she was relieved. Catherine looked up from her place on the couch, lips pressed into a straight line as she watched Lynn pass.

"So, are you gonna tell me what trouble you got yourself into last night, Missy? Or am I gonna have to keep guessing?"

"It doesn't matter now, Mom. It's over," Lynn said, shuffling to the stairs.

She gripped the banister, beginning her climb, when

Catherine said, "For now."

Lynn had chills. She assumed her mother was talking about the man who had spent the night, but on instinct, Lynn thought of the hospital, the ghosts, the woman who had died there, and wondered if it could all be over so easily.

Epilogue
Lynn

SEEING A PSYCHIATRIST was probably Lynn's least favorite thing to do, but it was worse this week. Under his gaze, Lynn squirmed and worried that all of her lies were on the surface of her skin, ready to be called out.

What was worse was that she wanted to spill her guts. To tell her about the connection with Victoria, and the moments where she'd seen Damien. They had felt so vital, so important, to her that she didn't like the idea of pretending she had never experienced them.

The worst part of it all was avoiding telling her about Jayden and the confusing mush of feelings that he inspired inside her. Those were the feelings she needed a psychiatrist for but revealing how she met him would mean having to tell the rest, so she stayed silent. The police had never come to talk to her about Jayden's deceased friends, and so she imagined the story he had woven hadn't mentioned her. If she drew a connection between them now, it would ruin everything.

When Lynn met back up with Amelia in the waiting room, she seemed especially anxious. Lynn was used to Amelia fawning over her, but she wasn't used to her hugging her for the hell of it.

"How'd it go?" Amelia asked as soon as they made

it to the parking lot.

"I didn't tell him anything about the hospital if that's what you're wondering."

"I figured you wouldn't, but I worried anyway." A pause. "So…how *are* you doing with all of it?"

Lynn looked away, using the excuse of opening the passenger side door instead of answering.

"That's okay. You don't have to talk about it yet, but I expect you to one day."

"Fine, *one* day," Lynn agreed, plopping into the seat with her arms folded across her chest. "But not today."

Amelia's shoulders slumped, but she didn't argue as she started the engine. Lynn stared out the window as her sister drove. As the scenery around them turned from the city to the rural backstreets of home, she found herself wondering about Jayden and where he was. Had he and his friend already gone home?

Maybe we'll meet again one day, his words bounced around the inside of her.

She had told herself not to dissect them, that assuming her own meaning wouldn't make anything better, but she thought about them almost constantly. Did that mean that he *wanted* to see her again even after knowing the worst parts of her?

The idea made her nervous, and nervous was *not* something she wanted to be.

"Are you cold?" Amelia asked.

Lynn shook her head but didn't bother to explain

herself. When they arrived back at home, Amelia led the way to the porch, hopping up the steps in graceful little hops. Lynn stayed at the bottom.

"If it's alright with you, I'm gonna hang here for a little while," Lynn said, plopping down onto the step.

Amelia frowned, and Lynn clenched her hands into fists, braced for her sister to try to coerce her into talking. "Okay. I'll be inside if you need me."

The door clattered behind her before Lynn let herself breathe. She stared into the woods thinking about Damien, the hospital, Victoria, and Jayden. She patted the wood of the step beside her, imagining it to be Damien's leg.

He's not coming back, one of her voices whispered cruelly.

She doubled over as if someone had hit her in the stomach. The pain of the comment was so real, so potent, that it dissolved her image, leaving her in tears.

You need to move on, he had told her.

He hadn't bothered to ask if she *wanted* to move on. Because she didn't, and even for Jayden's presence, she didn't think she could. No one would ever treat her the way Damien did.

What if... One of her voices pondered.

She couldn't decide if she hated that one more or the other one.

No what if... She argued back.

Ring.

The faint echo of the landline buzzed in the

background.

"Lynn!" Amelia called.

Lynn shut her eyes, bracing herself. No one ever called her, but when they did, she wondered *why.* She hated phone calls.

Damn debt collectors, she thought.

Soft footsteps announced Amelia's approach as she peeked her head out. "Hey, I know you need some time to decompress, but there's a message you might want to hear."

Lynn glanced at her sister, unsure if she should believe her or not. When Amelia didn't leave, Lynn sighed and got up, going back into the house. She glared at the phone the entire walk toward it and pressed play on the answering machine with far more force than necessary. The message started with a rushing whisper of wind, and she was ready to hang up when a voice finally started to speak.

"Hey, Lynn, it's Jayden. I got your number from the phone book. Anyway, I— uh, can we talk? If not, it's cool, but I guess, well, I wanted to let you know I'm here. If you want me to be."

A pause as more of the rushing air filtered through the phone.

"I guess that's it. Hopefully, I'll hear from you soon."

The message ended, but Lynn continued to stare at the answering machine as if she expected Jayden to crawl right through it. Her heart thundered as she replayed his words.

He wanted to talk to her? About what?

Her finger hovered above the call button, and she was tempted to let it ring, to hear Jayden's voice on the other end of the line, but she was afraid that she would say something wrong and hear that disappointment again.

She replayed the message instead. He sounded nervous and...*hopeful*? She liked the sound. It reminded her of the way Damien used to sound around her when they had first started dating one another.

With a painful twinge, she suddenly realized how much she missed that. What it felt like to have someone by her side.

The phone started to ring before she had realized she had gone through with it and pressed the button. Jayden didn't answer, and she hung up the phone, reaching up to press her palm against her forehead. She didn't know why she felt so foolish, but she did. She tried to tell herself it was a ridiculous reaction, but part of her had expected him to rush to answer the phone.

If she hadn't been able to face her family a few minutes ago, it was impossible now. She went back outside, glad Amelia had given her some privacy. She needed to go for a long walk, to think and escape like she used to do when she felt as if she had the weight of the world on her shoulders.

The walk down the vacant highway wasn't as peaceful as she'd hoped it would be. Not with the trees on either side threatening to pull her back into thoughts of the hospital and everything that had happened. Despite it all, part of her itched to seek out the building and make sure it had really burned down.

She was afraid. Afraid that their hard work wouldn't be the end of the curse, and that she'd be trapped all over again.

Lynn pulled her hood up as she rounded the bend, heading toward the ice cream shop. The bridge was nearby, and she froze, debating going over to it or continuing on her way. Eventually, the bridge won out, and she trotted over to it.

She ran her fingers along the locks until she found hers, the one she and Damien had hung up what felt like forever ago. Her thumb stroked the engravings, and she let go, listening to it clang back to the fence. She wished she had the key, wished she could unlock it and take it home with her, but it would stay forever.

Just like the destroyed remains of the asylum full of so many secrets.

The End

* * *

About the Author

Kayla Frederick is the new pen name for established author, Kayla Krantz. A little neurotic and a huge lover of Halloween, she enjoys creepy stories.

www.ingramcontent.com/pod-product-compliance
Lightning Source LLC
Chambersburg PA
CBHW030759190726
48285CB00003B/937